Pete & Shirley

The Great Tar Heel Novel

Clyde Edgerton • Lee Smith • Fred Chappell
David Guy • Tim McLaurin • Jill McCorkle
William McCranor Henderson
Kaye Gibbons • Jerry Bledsoe
Margaret Maron • Philip Gerard
Marianne Gingher • Bland Simpson
Laura Argiri • John Welter
Jaki Shelton Green • Michael Chitwood

Edited by David Perkins

A Down Home Press book in asociation with The *News & Observer*

Down Home Press, Asheboro, N.C.

ISBN 1-878086-49-9
Library of Congress Catalog Card No. 95-083311

This book is fiction. Any resemblance of characters in this work to people living or dead is purely coincidental. Anybody thinking that he or she resembles any of these characters should seek counseling immediately.

Printed in the United States of America

Cover illustration by Keith Simmons
Book design by Beth Glover

Down Home Press
P.O. Box 4126
Asheboro, N.C. 27204

To Caitlin, Dylan, Aaron, Ian,
Evan, Arla and Jenna
— the most fun in my life

— David Perkins

Contents

1
– Clyde Edgerton –
Open Secrets

As evening settled in, Hortense the nighthawk lifted silently from her comfortable nest and took to the graying sky over Cary, North Carolina. Interstate 40 was a favorite hunting ground. Fat mice abounded, thanks to the wide shoulders provided by the N.C. Dept. of Transportation.

Far to the west rose the hill that was Chapel Hill, closer — the pickle building of Durham. To the south and west the fingers of Jordan Lake grasped rolling hills from which rose the giant smoking chimney called Shearon Harris Nuclear Plant. Up to the north the Raleigh art tower glinted in the dusk.

Directly below, families turned off their sprinklers and prepared for supper — or more likely, dinner, nowadays — and evenings of love, hate, fear, hope, popcorn, "The Simpsons" and "Rescue 911."

"Pete!" Shirley called. "Honey! Come up here. See what I've found."

Shirley was sitting on the living room floor. She stood up slowly, looking down into a large cardboard box. She wiped the palms of her hands on the back pockets of her jeans.

Her husband, Pete, sat in an armless chair in the basement playing his guitar and working up a new country song, "Bring Your Bad Side to the Bed Side." He called it his "Grand Ole Comeback Song." Shirley called it something else. He'd been working on it for eight months now.

"What is it?" he said.

"Just come up here. I found something."

"'Bring your hot lips to the hayloft, bring your...'" he mumbled as he started up the stairs two at a time.

On the living room floor around the cardboard box lay several neatly folded sweaters. An overcoat and almost new gray tweed sports jacket — Pete's size, 44 Regular — lay across the coffee table.

"'Bring your biscuit mix to the stovetop...your...' Nah. What's up, babe?" Pete stuck his finger in his ear and shook his hand vigorously.

Shirley looked away. Cleaning his ears this way was one of his odd habits.

She pointed. "This is what's up."

They stood looking into the bottom of the box at a large burgundy vinyl briefcase. It lay flat, with long strips of duct tape encircling it, the ends of each strip meeting evenly near the latches. Taped to the side of the briefcase was an 8-by-11 piece of notebook paper on which was written, in black felt-tip marker: "Personal. Do Not Open Until After My Death and the Deaths of My Children. Donald Griffin."

"Oh, man," said Pete. He grabbed the briefcase by the handle, pulled it out, and set it on the floor. "I didn't even know he was dead!"

"You knew him?"

"You could say that. But I hadn't seen him for three years, ever since we ran into each other at the Jiffy Lube. Where'd you find this?"

"I was bored — looking for some fiction ideas — went to a garage sale."

"How about that? I guess we ought to get it back to him."

"He's dead."

"Well, I know that. But what about his wife?"

"Well...but it's mine now — ours."

"Why did you buy all this, Shirl?"

"Clothes. For you. I had no idea this was in it. Let's open it. Maybe it's a true crime story. Maybe the Mafia got him."

"No, I don't think we should open it." Pete picked up the briefcase. "Here, I'll put it somewhere. I mean just..." Pete started into their bedroom, turned abruptly, walked in a kind of dazed half circle. "I'll take care of it," he said. "I got to get back to my song, babe. I'm on a roll." He headed for the basement.

"Pete! Pete, what's the matter? Who was Mr. Griffin?"

Pete called over his shoulder: "One of my high school teachers, late '60s. Before your time, Shirl."

"Oh."

Pete Houser, 45, and Shirley Graves-Loggins, 39, of 1537 Fluffy Ridge Drive, had been married just over a year. Second marriage for each — three children, total, all away from home now. They lived in a whitewashed neocolonial ranch in Green Meadow Farms, a middle to upper-middle income subdivision between Apex and Cary, near MacGregor Downs, an upper middle-upper to lower upper-upper subdivision. In fact, they had their first date at MacGregor Downs at a Halloween party given by some of their mutual upper middle-upper friends. Pete had come as Herb Alpert with a low-cut Mexican shirt, Shirley as Miss Marple. When someone asked her to do a striptease, Shirley played along a little while Pete tooted reveille. There were a few sparks that night.

They met again a week later at an N.C. Association of Educators conference in its bermed building in Raleigh. Pete taught shop and vocational studies at Eastern High School just outside Apex. He was raised in Apex and graduated from Eastern High himself. Shirley had grown up in Cleveland and come south with her first husband and was now a guidance counselor at Cary High School. After her divorce, she had taken up fiction writing — and joined the writers' organization called CAW (Carolina Area Writers).

She missed very few readings and workshops in the Tri-angle. Nancy Oldsin of Pheasant Run Books had once introduced her to Fred Chappell.

When she and Pete were married, Shirley dropped her former husband's name and insisted on keeping her maiden name, hyphenated with her mother's maiden name. Pete said he had never especially liked all that feminist stuff but he guessed he could be flexible. Oh, they'd had the normal irritations and disagreements during their year of marriage, but this time around they had known better than to trust infatuation; they had each angled for sex and stability and found it. But sometimes, like now, Shirley wondered if she knew Pete at all. Something would come over him. Something about his past, it seemed.

After dinner, Shirley picked up the remote phone, took it into the bathroom, and called Delores, Pete's cousin. If anyone knew about this Mr. Griffin — or anybody else in town — it would be Delores.

"Delores, this is Shirley…"

In the basement, Pete opened the lid to the quilt trunk, checked to see if it might have a secret compartment. It didn't. He placed the briefcase in the bottom of the trunk, covered it with blankets and quilts, closed the lid, and sat down on it. He thought back to his high school years, and to one girl in particular, and even more particular to the sweat gleaming on her upper lip at those hot pre-football season band practices.

Upstairs: "Delores, I need to ask you something. Did you know a Mr. Griffin at Eastern High?"

"Oh, yes. The band director. Way back when. He was kind of Italian looking and always had alcohol on his breath. Good band director, though. Me and Pete were both in the band. We won some awards. Cary Band Day was one. Back when Cary was still Southern."

"Did Mr. Griffin ever seem like he had something to

hide? I'm just curious."

"Oh, yes sirree. There was a scandal. Didn't Pete tell you?"

"No, not exactly."

"That Pete. He's more like Uncle Melvin than Uncle Melvin hisself. They're both quiet types, and love to eat — and pee in the yard."

"Really? At the same time?"

"No, Uncle Melvin lives over in north Durham."

"I mean eat and pee at the same time."

"No. No, different times. They ain't got but two hands, silly. It runs in the family. 'Course now, occasionally they might eat and pee in the yard at the same time. Who knows?"

"What was the scandal — with Mr. Griffin?"

"I seem to remember he fell in love — head over heels — with Samantha, Samantha Lambert, yes, that was her name, the head majorette, and she got pregnant and all. I think. Or it seems like she did. And a gun was involved, and then it all got hushed up. It didn't really heat up until after I left for East Carolina, so I don't remember how it all ended up. Then I moved on to Baltimore and never got the straight of it. I do remember they said Mr. Griffin moon-lighted in a jazz band that played in the Frog and Nightin-gale, or whatever it was, on Medlin Drive."

Shirley imagined what might be in the briefcase. A journal? Letters? What a story! Band director and major-ette. Alcohol. Pregnancy. The scenario looked promising, brilliant even — for a short story, or maybe even a novel.

"One other thing," said Dolores. "Pete's best friend, Denny Baucom, dated Samantha. Denny played trumpet, and Mr. Griffin would take him and Pete home sometimes and they'd play Dixieland music. Pete was playing trom-bone, but they all three could play different instruments, and it seems to me like Samantha did some singing with them."

Downstairs, Pete was strumming his guitar, staring at the wall, his mind's eye watching a baton twirling high into the night sky, remembering the windows of his daddy's '60 Buick LeSabre all steamed up over there off the loop road on the back side of Lake Wheeler.

Upstairs: "Thanks, Delores. Talk to you later. Bye-bye."

Shirley was already thinking stories. She thought about her next day's CAW conference. On her session sheet she had selected "Planting Plot I," "Planting Plot II," "Lunch," "Open Mike" and "Free Time." Her best friend, Monica Jeffers, a poet, would be reading at open mike — or else Shirley would have selected "Planting Plot III."

If she knew what was in that briefcase, a journal or diary maybe, or journals and letters — and if she knew key elements of the story, and happened to run into the Planting Plot instructor, Fred Chappell, or one of the other famous writers, maybe even Leon Rooke, then she would certainly have something interesting to discuss with them.

At the top of the basement stairs, Shirley looked around for the briefcase. Pete must have taken it down with him. She looked down the stairs where she could see him bathed in the flickering green light of his computer screen, doing some nighttime travel on the Internet. "I'm going to bed, honey. Have you got the briefcase?"

"It's right here. Night-night, babe."

Before light the next morning, Shirley was in the basement, sitting on the quilt trunk. She'd found the briefcase. She reached for the end of a strip of duct tape. She pulled, and the tape made a kind of popping sound. She heard the door open at the top of the stairs. She saw Pete's bare feet, then his legs — in his light blue pajamas with the brown dog heads.

"Pete," she said. "I'm down here. I was just thinking about…You look like you haven't slept much, honey."

2
– Lee Smith –
She of All My Dreams

"You got that right." Pete's familiar witticism sounded mostly forlorn. The strange sad note in his voice made Shirley drop the briefcase like a hot potato and charge up the stairs two at a time to hurl herself at her husband. Now Shirley was not a small person, more than an armful. Her onslaught propelled Pete backward, his arms flailing like a dog-head windmill, down the hall and into the bedroom and onto the comfy king-size bed.

"How about a little ooh-poo-pa-doo?" she whispered euphemistically into his very clean ear.

And soon the two were lost in passion, or as close to passion as it is possible to get in Cary, and when it was all over, Shirley sat propped up on one elbow and watched the pearly light of dawn gradually illumine Pete's sweet slack-jawed sleeping face. Oh, Pete! It seemed like only yesterday that Shirley had placed that fateful ad in *The Independent's* personals:

> **BUILT FOR COMFORT NOT FOR SPEED**
>
> *Creative, compassionate, old-fashioned DWF, 40, big blue eyes, big blonde hair, kind heart, ISO that special someone to share everything the Triangle has to offer. Recovering fundamentalist loves line-dancing, cooking, BOMC, dogs, cats, the Angus Barn, outlets and 'Mystery!' on PBS. Hates cappuccino and walks on beach. No drugs, no vegetarians please.*

15

Shirley's friend Monica had told her she shouldn't put in that last part. "Everybody likes to walk on the beach!"

But Shirley really didn't like to walk too much in general, especially not at the beach, where you had to use muscles that were better left alone, giving you cramps in the back of your calves. Shirley would rather look at the beach from a room at the Whaler Inn, say, while sipping a margarita, which was just one of many things she had learned about since her divorce from old No-Frills Frank, the man to whom fun was anathema. When Frank gave her those battery cables for their 20th anniversary, Shirley saw the writing on the wall. So she followed her bliss to Cary, where she got a job, placed the ad and was soon showered with responses. It was clear that a lot of people were also out there looking for love.

Shirley had no trouble turning down **YOUNG STAL- LION, NINTH STREET NURTURER, MALE NURSE IN NEED, P.C. PLAYMATE, DOMINANT MALE,** or **DUKE DECONSTRUCTIONIST**. She hesitated over **GARNER DREAMBOAT, CHATHAM COUNTY SIXTIES PERSON** and **CAROLINA FAN**. Finally she called **COUNTRY BOY**.

"I just wanna know one thing," Pete said in that slow deep voice she would soon grow to love. "What's BOMC? Burlington Manufacturers Outlet Center?"

"No, it's *The Bridges of Madison County*," Shirley replied. "My favorite book."

Pete said that he himself was not much into reading but that he was going to a Halloween party in MacGregor Downs that night, and he wondered if Shirley would like to go with him.

"I'll meet you there," she said instantly, figuring that it's always better for a girl to have her own car. And the rest is history.

"History." The word reminded Shirley of those pages from the past still waiting for her in the basement. She got out of bed and tiptoed down the stairs.

The mysterious briefcase turned out to be bursting

with old spiral notebooks (the kind everybody used in high school) and sheet music, plus one pair of wadded-up pantyhose, two brilliant blue tassels of the sort to be found on majorette boots, a corsage of dried rosebuds, several knee socks which did not match, three high school year-books, a single-shot .38 revolver and over 50 Peppermint Patty wrappers carefully pressed out flat and saved in a little stack.

What in the world!?

Gingerly, Shirley plucked out the pantyhose and deposited them in a trash can. Now she could see the shiny gun more clearly, nestling there in the knee socks. Was it loaded? No way to tell. Shirley held her breath as she reached in and grasped it firmly, keeping its ominous little snout pointed away from her. She placed it carefully on the shelf which held all her craft materials and then stood there studying it, her heart beating wildly. Of course, she should tell Pete about this. She should tell him right now. But something kept her from doing it. Pete would just take over, she knew he would. And Shirley wanted more time with that briefcase. She wanted to read all those notebooks.

Shirley took a deep breath, remembering what she had learned in the "Women Who Run With Wolves" course she took from that holistic woman in Carrboro. "Live like your hair's on fire," the woman said. Actually this is exactly what Shirley had been doing ever since she left Frank, and it was no time to stop now. Shirley covered up the gun with one of those macrame ducks she used to make back before she took up writing. OK.

Shirley sat back down on the trunk and pulled several of the notebooks out of the briefcase. Then she fished a few Pepperidge Farm Goldfish out of the pockets of her robe, where she liked to keep them in case of a snack attack. Nibbling, she opened a green notebook. The handwriting was large and florid, like signatures of presidents. She began to read at random.

Sept. 3, 1966:

I am all shook up. I am in the grip of something larger than myself here, and I do not know how it will all end, or if it will at all. I have not been seized by such feeling since those long-ago undergraduate days in Chapel Hill, when I used to sneak into Hill Hall in the dead of night and play Wagner on the grand piano until dawn, when — drenched with sweat and overcome with emotion — I wandered out onto Franklin Street in a daze of art and youth. Ah, those were the days indeed — those halcyon days when I was going to be a concert pianist and composer of international renown, when women were going to follow me from triumph to triumph, and all the world was going to open for me like a brilliant flower...Such delusion! Such bitter folly!

I see it all so clearly now, and yet here I am, artist manque, so many years later, trapped in a dead-end job and a loveless marriage, teaching teenagers to play "The Star-Spangled Banner" year after year while inside I smolder in vain.

Until today, that is.

May this date be forever emblazoned across Carolina's bright blue sky!

For it is today that SHE showed up, SHE, the eternal archetypal SHE of all my dreams.

Hot stuff! But Pete would be waking up any minute now. Quickly, Shirley put everything except two of the notebooks back in the briefcase, taped it up again, and left it on top of the quilt trunk, exactly as it had been when Pete discovered her there with it. Now he would never know. What was he so worried about, anyway?

By the time he woke up, she was back in bed beside him, and he greeted her with a big kiss.

"That's my girl!" he said.

But later that very morning, Shirley couldn't keep from grinning as she patted the notebook beside her on the seat. "Fred Chappell, eat your heart out!" she said to herself, on her way to the CAW conference.

3
– Fred Chappell –
Snakehandling

But it seemed that something had already eaten Chappell's heart out — or his brains, anyhow. "Planting Plot I," the hour-long session of the Carolina Area Writers convention given over to the direction of the old Tar Heel scribbler, had been designed to teach authors like Shirley Graves-Loggins some of the basics of plot construction. But in Chappell's trembling hands it had become...well, Shirley couldn't describe what it had become. The bleary-eyed instructor poured words — "Aristotle," "syllabic achronicity," "Cthulhu," "Homeric simile," "grandmother" — upon his bemused audience like a man slopping Pulitzer Prize-winning hogs. A gray-haired woman on Shirley's left whispered that she didn't think the speaker was quite sober — and received a response from a woman behind her:

"Well, he never has been."

"Have you seen him before?"

The good-looking blonde replied: "Every day for 35 years. He's my husband."

Shirley sat to the end of this daft performance. Being from Cleveland, she was concerned to show good manners among these Southerners who prided themselves on politeness. Yet she need not have been so meticulous. As she left she found that the crowd had dwindled to only herself and two unshaven dozing young men. All the listeners, including Mrs. Chappell, had slipped away.

So she moved on to the next session, "Planting Plot II," with barren expectations and was warmly surprised to

21

find the presentation sensible, well-ordered and helpful. The speaker was a young man with a strong jaw-line and an expression as intense as a sizzling dynamite fuse. He spoke of characterization, of incident and detail, of setting and background in clear and useful terms. His imagery only added bite to his remarks.

Writers are oviparous, he explained. Like snakes. They produce eggs outside their maternal sac. Then they leave them alone to hatch. He told them that, like snakes shedding their skins, plots had to renew themselves. A good writer never lets an idea escape, he said; he is always lying in wait, ready to strike and secure his prey – that is, his subject.

Shirley's stomach rumbled. Do they get a week to digest it? Shirley wondered.

"I'll show you what I mean," he said. He opened one of the six plastic foam chests flanking his podium and pulled out a large gray snake. "This is a water moccasin," he said. "If I can get him poised to strike, you'll see my point."

Like the smooth skeletal undulation of a prowling python, a murmur of consternation ran through the mostly female audience.

"Don't worry," said Tim McLaurin. "I used to make my living with these creatures." He was referring to the traveling circus sideshow he'd given up to write books. "But I'll always love them for what they've taught me." He laid the snake on the table and poked it with his finger, but the reptile ignored him. "He's tired," the author announced. "I've been carrying him around for shows at nursery schools and mental wards. Let's try something else." But as he turned to restore the moccasin to its chest his foot tangled with a table leg and he pitched forward, dropping the one snake and toppling three chests onto the floor. "Oops," he said.

The lids flew open and out slithered what seemed to Shirley hundreds of snakes. Of course, there were only a few score, but Shirley's black terror had rattled her arithmetical abilities.

The air was so filled with shrieks, squeaks, squeals and screams it sounded like the immolation scene from an Indonesian opera. McLaurin tried to calm the crowd.

"They're just copperheads," he called. "Most of them aren't even fully mature."

Another shriek.

He reached for another chest. "Look," he said. "These kingsnakes'll take care of some of the copperheads." He dumped out a clump of long, brightly colored serpents that wriggled quickly away.

Shirley scurried to the exit as fast as her wobbly knees would carry her.

"Wait now," Tim McLaurin was saying. "There's a lesson to be learned here — if you get too many writers involved in one project, they may get out of control."

But the room was empty and silent, except for the chafing of reptilian scales upon burgundy carpet. Shirley's session sheet now indicated lunch, but she knew she couldn't keep anything on her stomach. She wanted, she decided, a Jack Daniel's to calm her nerves, and headed for the lounge on the first floor of the Carolina Inn. Her need for a curative was not unique; the bar was crowded with writers, editors, teachers and poets. The hubbub made a sound like the surf breaking on Wrightsville Beach — except for the occasional shriek of some unobservant soul.

She got a drink and turned to survey the room. Yonder stood Lee Smith in a cowgirl outfit, charming a circle of goggle-eyed menfolk. Jerry Bledsoe chatted with a famous ax-murderess. Behind her Shirley heard the phrase "Cthulhu Homeric grandmother" droned in a low mumble and turned to see Fred Chappell at the bar, giving the dazed barkeep a full account of his "Planting Plot" speech. He seemed oblivious to the three snakes coiled around his ankles.

He sees them all the time, Shirley thought. He doesn't know these are real.

"Shirley Graves-Loggins!"

She turned to acknowledge the greeting and found

her friend, the poet Monica Jeffers, looking at her in happy surprise.

"Monica! I was just going to hear you at the open mike."

"I won't be there," Monica said. "Since I became a New Formalist they won't let me perform."

"Why not?"

"They're jealous. I've gone into country music, and they can't stand the competition. Listen to my new song," she said. "I just wrote it this morning:

"Bring your bad side to my bed side,
"Bring your honey side to my bread side,
"Bring your hillside to my sled side,
"And we'll go down together."

As she heard these words, something clicked in Shirley's mind. Well, it wasn't really a click, but a sound more like that of a dirty sock dropping into a vat of sorghum molasses. Hadn't she heard these phrases before? Hadn't Pete been singing them this morning? How had Monica got hold of the words?

4
– David Guy –
Assertiveness Training

But Monica continued to recite her song in the crowded lounge:

"Drive your ball straight down my fairway

"And I'll drive your every care away

"Come to the top of my stairway

"And we'll go down together."

From a group near them, a tall balding man, already redfaced, turned to speak.

"What lovely imagery," he said. "I'm touched."

"Thank you," Monica said. "You're an editor?"

"Just a poet, like yourself. Maybe we could have a drink and…mix our metaphors."

Monica frowned. "Didn't you see my button?"

On the gentle slope of her left breast was a blue button featuring fiery red letters: TRASH.

"Some reference to your background?" He brightened. "Your moral standards?"

"Triangle Radicals Against Sexual Harassment, twerp."

The man blanched. This woman had given every appearance of being a Chapel Hill Earth Mother. Apparently she was from Durham.

"Now take a hike," Monica said, "or you'll be singing soprano in the Durham Boys Choir."

The tall, balding poet wobbled away.

"That's what I hate about these writers' conferences," Monica said. "All the guys hitting on you."

Monica was — as Shirley's father back in Cleveland would have said — a piece of work. She really was Shirley's best friend, was in some ways a role model for her. They had met at the "Women Who Run With Wolves" course (which had confirmed Shirley's general hypothesis about such gatherings: If you have the nerve to show up for assertiveness training, you don't need it). Monica didn't just live like her hair was on fire, her hair *was* on fire, bright red and curly and sticking out all over. She was taller than Shirley, her fair skin sprinkled with freckles, and she was put together — again, as Shirley's father would have said — like a brick outhouse.

But it was Monica's nerve that Shirley really admired, her sheer brass. It was Monica who had urged Shirley to run an Indy personal, and when the replies had come rolling in — her voice mail had gone TILT! Monica said, "Go out with all of them. You'll be lucky to find one who's any good."

Monica was what Shirley thought of as a real Durham woman. She hung out on Ninth Street, sat in the bleachers at the Bulls games, had even shot a game of snooker at the Broad Street Green Room. She and Shirl — as Monica called her — had really bonded during a weekend at the beach, when they stuffed themselves with fried clams at the Sanitary, played miniature golf at Jungleland, tried that game where you hit the gophers with the hammer (Shirley was always too slow, but Monica whacked a dozen), then went back to the Whaler Inn and drank margaritas far into the night. At 4 a.m. they had walked together on the fishing pier, way out where only the king fishermen go. One old salt had brightened at their approach but backed off when he saw the fire in Monica's eye.

What Shirley had realized that night, as they talked of literature and of life, was that a woman like Monica was just what she needed to give her courage in her writing career. She didn't agree with all of Monica's attitudes — she wished she'd lighten up on men, for instance — but she loved her strength.

Monica had reached into her bag, pulled out an un-filtered Camel and actually struck a match before she remembered where she was. "Go ahead, shoot me at sunrise!" she yelled at the people staring at her all over the room. "I hate Chapel Hill," she said as she dropped the cigarette back in her bag.

"I'm starved," she said, rummaging through the bag. "I've had a rough morning." Shirley couldn't help wondering what had been so rough about it.

Finally Monica found the miniature candies she'd been looking for and offered one to Shirley. "Peppermint Patty?" The words struck a dull gong in Shirley's subconscious. Wasn't it Peppermint Patties that had — so to speak — cemented the relationship between Samantha and the band director?

"Where'd you get that first line of your song?" Shirley said, out of the blue.

"First lines!" Monica said. "Who knows where they come from? The depths of the subconscious. A rhythm in the blood. Maybe we pluck them out of the air."

Or out of your best friend's husband's mouth, Shirley thought. After it's been all over yours.

"The way a poem comes together," Monica said. "I could talk about it forever."

"I have to go to the bathroom," Shirley said.

She managed to make it out of the room before the tears came. She knew one thing. If Pete had been fooling around with Monica, his ooh-poo-pa-doo was ooh-poo-pa-done.

She found the ladies room, locked herself in a toilet stall, sat on the seat and took the notebook out of her bag. She had the feeling that the key to her husband's behavior was in his past, and she leafed through the notebook until she found a reference to him. It didn't take long.

Sept. 14: The boys over for a jam session. Old Hot Lips Baucom was hitting the high ones, but Houser was all thumbs as usual. I wish he could play like he can eat. Three plates of the old lady's lasagna, after he'd already had a chicken fried steak at home. He's one of these North Carolina lunks. I can just see him 30 years from now, sitting around with his fat wife.

She hadn't even been fat in 1961! Shirley thought. And criticizing Pete's playing! Something in Griffin's attitude made her rally to her husband's side. Pete was a good old North Carolina boy, even if his new wife did have to get his favorite dishes from the takeout window. He liked a soft, warm, cuddly woman, not one of those gopher-whackers like Monica.

Samantha came to pick up Baucom, eating her favorite candy. Oh, to be that Peppermint Patty! My only hope is that Baucom wore his lips out on the trumpet. The funny thing is, I thought she kind of had her eyes on Houser. She gave him some of her candy. Like he needed it.

There! Samantha knew a good man when she saw one.
Samantha? She gave him candy?
In bewilderment, and still in pain, Shirley glanced at the wall beside her. A limerick had been written there.

If you'll let me be the instigator,
I'll be your Great Emancipator,
Push the button in my elevator,
And we'll go down together.

Shirley stared dumbly. How many people were writing this song? Maybe the words really were floating around in the air.

Just then — the door to the outside had opened and closed several times — a small copperhead slithered under the door of Shirley's stall. She stifled a shriek: She knew she shouldn't show fear. St. Francis would have spoken gently to the little reptile. In her sweetest, sexiest voice, she said, "Aren't you in the wrong place, little fella?"

"Maybe so, lady," said a voice outside the stall. "I just came in here after my snake."

5
– Tim McLaurin –
Gone Fishing

Pete hooked another minnow through the back. He was fishing for crappie, deep in Lake Jordan, where the currents were still warm. Three nice fish were already in the cooler. In the hills across the lake he could see the roads being cut for fine new houses with a lake view. A few yards directly beneath, the Haw River had once flowed over rocks beside a small secluded meadow, before the dam was built. Today the water was mostly calm and as cloudy as the sky. Pete liked the flat gray color after the explosions in his sleep the night before.

God, those dreams! The images of three people he thought he had pickled and put away forever back in his drinking days had whirled through his sleep like a runaway movie.

Denny, with that eternal, dumb grin on his face, clear blue eyes, the leader of the team in touchdowns his senior year…

Griffin, his brooding, black eyes and thick hair longer than any of the other male teachers, the heartthrob of every female student…

And Samantha, twirling like a bright tornado, skirt high on her thighs, that baton soaring under the stadium lights like a pure white dove.

Wafting between these portraits had been sounds and smells — the throb of jazz music after their combo had started to get good, Denny's trumpet blending with the strings, Samantha crooning in that sultry soprano of hers,

31

and the sweet-pungent smoke hanging over Griffin's rumpus room. Samantha would roll that peppermint across her tongue, her eyes closed, and Pete would find just the right note to explain it all.

River water over the rocks on the Haw, the wind in willow branches on those lost days at the meadow. Ripping through the images and odors Pete heard again the dull thud of shoulder pads and clapping hands — and the awful crack of a pistol shot. He felt again the jolt of a fist against his face, tasted blood.

Pete cast his line again, and in the ripples he thought of Shirley. He imagined her at the writers' conference, men and women jammed together, trying to each create a world that doesn't exist. He felt a bit of disdain for his wife's new passion and for her writer friends. Always gabbing about plot and pacing and resolution — world and lives tightly controlled and moving toward a manicured ending. From what Pete had seen and felt in his own years, real life was mostly hope and chance. He hadn't rolled many sevens.

Bring me your heart of hunger,
and banquet on the feast of love.

Pete hadn't remembered that line in years. It was from a song he and Denny had written back when their music was beginning to reflect the folk influence. The lyrics came more easily back then, but he was still writing about the same thing.

A breeze wrinkled the water, and Pete thought back to that morning. He had gotten up early to watch cartoons, hoping they'd shut off the images and smells of the night before. Then, after Shirley left for Chapel Hill, he'd gone downstairs to gather his fishing tackle. The briefcase was still inside the quilt chest, but it had been turned another way, as if some energy inside had spun the bag around. On a shelf above the window sat a stack of seven red plastic A.A. chips. Why had he saved them? Seven times he'd gone dry, six times he'd fallen off the wagon. Those years between chips had cost him a wife, built a wall between himself and his friends. Those years had also cost him any chance at a career in music.

Pete's rod gave a pull. He pulled back, then reeled in another flapping crappie. Even in the pewter daylight, the fish scales reflected color, and for a few seconds the images started again:

Denny shook Pete's hand, then held it for several seconds, grinning as always, looking sharp as a razor in his Marine uniform. Both his cheeks were smeared with lipstick, and Samantha's eyes were shiny with tears. At the plane's doorway, Denny had turned and saluted them. His last letter from Nam had contained a four-leaf clover....

A fish tail drummed against the boat deck, and Pete heard the beep of a hospital machine measuring Samantha's pulse....

The crappie bounded into the air and flipped and fell with a thud against the boards, and Pete saw that last jab that backed Griffin up. They stood in the meadow by the lake, face to face, both with skinned knuckles and bleeding lips, standing slump-shouldered and too tired to punch any more.

"You swear it," Pete growled, spitting blood. "You swear it now on your honor if you have any left."

"I swear," Griffin said.

Pete unhooked the fish and dropped it in the cooler, then began to rebait. They had all gone down to the meadow in the middle of spring their senior year. Graduation was only a month away. Everyone got into the right frame of mind, then jammed for an hour. They were relaxing and looking at the clouds when Samantha stood and walked down to the riverbank. Pete heard a cry. It might have been a bird. Denny and Griffin were deep in their thoughts. Pete stood and walked to the river and found Samantha sitting on a rock, staring at her hand. A single drop of blood gleamed upon her white skin.

"I reached into the water for a pebble, and something cut me." She held out her arm.

"It was probably just a piece of quartz. Quartz can be sharp as glass."

At that moment, in midstream, a snake looped his way down the current and disappeared beyond the edge of a rock.

Samantha's eyes grew wide. "A snake could have bit me, Pete."

"It wasn't a snake. Anyway, that was a water snake. They're not poisonous."

"What if it was a cottonmouth?"

"It wasn't, Sam. There aren't any around here."

Samantha stood. She lifted her finger to Pete's lips. He stared at the drop of blood, then took her finger in this mouth and sucked gently at the wound. He tasted salt, and his head spun, and the gravel beneath their feet suddenly turned to quicksand.

6
– Jill McCorkle –
Epiphany on I-40

For once Shirley was relieved to get into that okra-colored Pinto that Frank had so generously let her keep in the divorce settlement and throw the piece of crap into gear. CAW was supposed to be a rewarding experience, a time and place for her creative energies to seek new avenues, but it had become a drag. She sped out onto the road, glancing briefly in the rearview to see Monica still standing in the middle of a group talking her blazing fool head off. For somebody who claims active membership in TRASH, Monica seemed to invite, incite, excite, for St. Peter's sake, any idiot who might have the energy to hit on her.

How did Monica know Pete's song? The question was driving Shirley out of her mind, and she was ready to grab Monica and force it out of her, except that all day long Monica conveniently had a crowd surrounding her; it would have been easier to have a heart-to-heart with Mother Teresa, which Monica surely was not.

Shirley suspected that there wasn't a pack of wolves on the face of the Earth who would want Monica running with or after them. The Junior League didn't want her, and Pete had once said that he couldn't imagine the man who might want her forever. Forever. Now why did he say that? Did that mean that he could imagine wanting her for a day or two?

Shirley had yet to figure out how Monica paid for that week at the Blockade Runner where she ate fancy seafood and gave birth to several litters of haiku, three sonnets and a whole notebook full of words that rhyme (the seeds of her future creations, she said), not to mention where she got the money for her silicone procedure and that brand new Lincoln Continental, which is certainly NOT the kind of car a young modern-minded woman might choose for herself, though it does have considerable leg room, especially if somebody was to want to do-wop-sha-bam in it.

When they first got together, Pete used to love to do things in the car that Shirley found cute but extremely uncomfortable. If only he had driven a Lincoln instead of a GM Pacer, they could have beat the band without all those muscular pains that had at various times driven them both into the strong hands of Hank Hodges, chiropractor, who has put up a billboard on the farmland off the side of I-40 with his picture and lots of promises about how he could cure cancer and diabetes with a little twist of your spine.

Shirley was passing his sign right this minute and she had a sudden urge to fly off the road and slam into his propaganda; she wanted to stomp on her brake and let somebody rear-end her so that the Pinto would burst into flames with that faulty gas tank everybody knows that it has.

And why hadn't Pete ever thought of getting her a new car? "You know why I love you, Shirley Poo?" he crooned way back, the gear shift knob digging into her thigh as she lay on top of her beloved whose torso was in the back seat and long legs were sprawled all over the dash. "Because your car makes mine look good!" Now it gave her a chill to think of that. Who was he? And what all was he doing in the basement all by himself? You were forever hearing of things happening in basements. Just pick up a newspaper and read it for yourself. Basements were horrible places, scary and seedy. And this area was full of them.

Shirley's heart was beating so fast that the Pinto couldn't keep up. She had let her foot press right on up to 70, and now the whole car was doing the shimmy shake so bad that she pulled into the breakdown lane to catch her breath. She was having what somebody at CAW once referred to as an epiphany. For a while everybody at CAW was having them. They had them in the bathtub and in the dental chair; they had them when they smelled popcorn and cut grass at the first football games. Monica said she had an enormous one that morning when she woke to find her parakeet stretched out stone dead on the floor of its little cage.

Up until this moment Shirley had thought that an epiphany might be something you ate — like a biscotti. That was when she whipped out the old dictionary only to discover that it was a name for the experience that for years she had marked by slapping herself in the head and saying "I coulda had a V-8!"

But now she was having one, a *bona fide* certified epiphany. Pete always liked to play band music when they fooled around in the car. Oh, dear Lord in heaven and keeper of the Pinto drivers! It was on more than one occasion that they danced the love dance to something or other by John Philip Sousa. When Pete proposed, "Hail to the Chief" was playing in the background. She would say, "Can't we play Sinatra or Elvis or the Beatles or something?" But no, it had to be band music. It had to be in the car. He liked it when she wore socks with a skirt. He once said she looked just like a high school girl. A high school girl!

Shirley gripped the steering wheel so that her hands would stop shaking only to look up into the eyes of yet another gigantic man on a billboard. This one promised that if she got bitten by a dog, if she slipped on her neighbor's driveway, if her spouse was unfaithful that there MIGHT be money in it. She thought of that pitiful man, Wilson in *The Great Gatsby*, whom Mr. Chappell had once referred to and how he looked into the eyes of God, and she had another one: two epiphanies in a half-hour! Did Fitzgerald ever have that many?

Pete was unfaithful. Either he was having an affair

right now or he had spent their entire marriage pretending that she was that little baton twirler or both! She had to devise a plan of discovery and then a plan of action, but first she had to get that Loretta Lynn song about "If my husband picks up trash he puts it in the garbage can" out of her head. She was hearing it to the beat of "You're a Grand Old Flag." Then she heard it to the beat of Pete's new song. And then she had an olfactory experience like she heard described on the Psychic Channel: She smelled peppermint so strong it made her eyes water, and with this odor came her own creative energy. She pulled back on the highway and sang her own song:

> "You bought yourself a Bronco and
>   left me with a Pinto.
> "You stallion, you stud, you ass.
> "Do you think you're O.J.?
> "Do you think that's OK?

> "Well, I sure as hell don't."

7

– William McCranor Henderson –
Burning Bridges

Shirley had once listened in horror as a woman on "Oprah" described how it felt to come home to an adulterous hubby with the words KILL, KILL, KILL crowding out every other thought in her head. Now she stood at the bottom of the basement stairs, arms folded across her belly, wondering what she was about to do next and whether it would end her up on "Oprah" someday. The TV was yammering in the next room — Pete was in there (she could smell his Brut) watching the fishing channel, some tobacco-mouthed dude jawing away over bluefish or blackfish or blowfish. KILL, KILL, KILL —

"Turn it off!" she said, thrusting herself into full view.

Pete's body didn't budge, but the screen went off, pooping to gray, with a little white blob in the middle getting teenier and teenier, like whatever giblet of hope and desire had kept them together for over a full year.

"You've been hot-diggety-dogging Monica."

"What —? I never touched her in my life!"

Sex goblins flittered through Shirley's head. There was a huge principle here: Hadn't Jesus laid it out in the Sermon on the Mount?

"In your mind you did, didn't you? In your heart."

Pete cleared his throat two or three times. "In my heart...Y'mean like Jimmy Carter? Well, that's possible I guess. Maybe you got that right."

She hadn't counted on this — bald-faced candor. "Wait a second here, Mr. Righteous — don't try to confess

39

to me!" she shouted, desperate not to lose her edge. "Who do you think you are, Jimmy Swaggart?"

"— Carter, Carter."

"Oh, stop it."

"Just kidding — golly, Shirl, can't we keep this light?" He stuck his finger in his ear.

"Light? ADULTERY, light? Is that what you're saying?"

Pete shifted uneasily in the bean bag chair.

"Come on, honey, there hasn't been anything like that. I met her once, at the Rod & Gun Firing Club range, while you were off at some book signing — but as far as anything else goes.... Well, maybe once or twice I've thought about her that way. But if a damn Baptist president of the United States can confess to *Playboy* about lustin' in his heart, what does it amount to?"

"If you think it...you've done it."

"Aw, come on —"

"That's what Jesus said!"

"Jesus is not involved here." Pete struggled to assume a dignified perch on the rolling sea of bean bag chair. "Listen, you want to be married to somebody perfect, go find Mister Rogers. I said I never touched her — and even just for the sake of argument, supposin' I did? That would make me no worse than 52 percent of American men as a whole, according to *The N&O.*"

"Oh, 52 wrongs out of a hundred makes a right? Don't insult my intelligence!" Shirley ran a furious hand through her hair.

"Well, hey, Shirl, if you want to go that route — the stud in *Bridges of Madison County* does it, and 20 zillion book buyers think HE's cool!"

'Don't you use BOMC against me, don't you dare! Anyway, there's no comparison. He's not married —"

"But SHE is — it's still adultery."

"It's not the same, it's not! He has a flat stomach, OK? You don't. He says simple, wise things, and you don't.

He's got the biggest love turn-on of all, which you DON'T."

"Now wait a minute —"

"High self-esteem."

"Oh, that—" Pete snorted. "He's satisfied with himself? Well, so would I be, if all I had to do was drift around Ohio — or Idaho or wherever it was — taking postcard shots of scuzzy old bridges and pleasing emotionally starved women —"

"You couldn't please an emotionally starved load of gravel."

"Well, fine, but does that qualify him to go off with any ol' body's wife? What's so morally wonderful about that? Huh?"

Shirley hung fire. How did he always do this — end up in the right?

"Well, he does one thing REAL good, Pete! And not splayed out on the floor of a GM Pacer like some big jellyfish the tide washed up —"

"How do you know?"

"I READ THE BOOK!"

"Well, y'oughta stay away from biographies!" He struggled up out of the bean bag chair and looked straight at her.

"It's...not...a...biography," she chanted, squeezing her teeth together.

"Well, it's all about that stuck-up guy with the gray hair weave, isn't it?"

"That's the author, idiot. It's fiction. He made it up."

Pete's lip curled in derision. "You're tryin' to tell me the author made it up — about himself? That's ridiculous."

A flood of red tide overwhelmed her brain. Then came the third epiphany of the day: The gun, the pistol from Griffin's time-capsule, was right where she had hidden it, under the macrame rabbit. Go for it! a voice yipped inside her head. As she lunged toward the craft shelf, she saw Pete's startled eyes following her. She lifted the rabbit, reached under it, and flourished the .38 revolver.

"Aw, Shirl, no. No! Not that —" Pete fell heavily to his knees.

"It's when I think of you and Monica," she half-sobbed, half-spat, "— working on that song together —" She pointed the gun at him awkwardly. "And don't tell me THAT happened inside your head! How DID it happen, by the way?"

"On the Internet, the Internet! There's this songwriters newsgroup and Monica's on it, too. About 50 of us. We've been trying come up with something that'll win Dave 'The Caveman' Pickens' songwriting contest on WEEB."

"Dave the...what?"

"Hell, honey, hasn't she talked to you about it? What do you think I'm doing at night when I sit down at the Mac with my guitar — singing it to sleep?"

Shirley peered at the lethal weapon in her hand. She hadn't the slightest idea how to make it fire — and even if she had, she realized suddenly, how could she do violence to this man? No matter what he had done — poor, poor Pete, she loved him so. She let the gun fall to the floor.

Then they were in each other's arms, moaning, whooping, sniffling, and finally just clinging.

"So you don't...lust after Monica?"

"No more than you lust after that flat stomach. And, by the way, a round stomach is more fun —"

"You got that right," Shirley let herself chuckle. "But what about...Samantha? What I read said she had her eye on you and pumped you full of Peppermint Patties and so on —"

"Ancient history, honey. Griffin was a jealous type. How much more of those diaries did you read, anyway?"

She puffed a sigh. "Mostly just that — plus the part where he goes on about Samantha as some sort of love goddess and whatnot, I don't know. Should I keep on reading?"

Pete's face toughened into an Old Testament frown. "Listen to me, Shirl, trust me now. You've got to hand over those diaries, OK? There's obviously some kind of a major curse on this stuff, and I want it out of our lives for good."

Shirley scowled at the three spiral notebooks in her tote bag. "What are you going to do?"

"We're going to have a bonfire and burn the whole nine yards."

"Burn the damned gun, too."

Outside, Pete collected some dust rags, cardboard boxes, busted cedar shingles, stacked them in the barbecue and sprayed them with charcoal starter. He glanced back at the house — Shirley's face wasn't watching from any aperture — lit a match and, closing his eyes, felt the satisfying WHUMP of conflagration. Then he carefully wrapped the real stuff in a canvas tarp and stashed it in the trunk of the Pinto — except the notebook that was labeled June-August 1967. This he took into the bathroom. Locking the door, he sat on the toilet and riffled the pages in search of one particular day — July 16, 1967.

And there it was.

8
– Kaye Gibbons –
Revelation

After locking the bathroom door, Pete sat down and read everything he feared was in Griffin's diary:

> July 16, 1962:
> I was fixing the toilet. Marsha leaning all over my shoulder asking me what was wrong. Fight ensued because somehow the rusted chain became my fault, something I had personally caused to occur to rattle her. Aaron Copland never had to deal with a rusted toilet chain or a wife all over him. Or teaching driver's ed in summer school. She finally said I was giving her a sick headache and went to bed.
>
> Thank God she was asleep when the phone rang. Samantha. She'd never called me at home before. Sounded urgent. I had to meet her in the band room right then. Wouldn't say why. I just had to go. Left a note on Marsha's bedside table saying I'd gone to the hardware store. She's already suspicious. Sees every female student as a threat. And that just makes her eat more. Already shaped like an outsized pear and getting broader. Not like Samantha. Sweet, lithe Sam.
>
> I drove to school as quickly as I could, and she was already there, having used the key I made for her. Had on pedal pushers and

a little cropped top. Like a fine, lean farm girl. She had ridden her bike. Hair lank from sweat. Purse strapped across her chest. She was shaking. I made her sit down, and I pulled a chair in front of her and smoothed her hair.

She said, "I'm late." She wouldn't look me in the eye.

Stupidly, I asked, "Late for what?"

"Don't joke," she said. Now she looked straight at me.

My eyes moved automatically to her stomach.

"How late?" I wanted to know.

"Late enough to know. I can't go to a doctor. He'll call my parents. But I know. A person knows."

"Maybe it's stress," I ventured. "They say stress can cause it."

"No," she said. "I figured it out on the calendar."

"What're you going to do?"

"I want to get married." She smiled at me. "I want to finish school and we can get married."

She was seeing me leaving Marsha, renting a little white house with a fence, going for walks with a stroller. I felt so sorry for her, loved her so deeply, that jealousy scarcely crossed my mind. But I had reason to be jealous. She wanted an answer.

"We need to think about this," I told her. Was I willing to take credit? Did I love her that much?

She let go of my hands and crossed her arms over her chest. "I've thought about it," she declared. "You have a responsibility."

I'd thought about it, too. Marsha's parents had money to send me to graduate school, and I'd stayed with her mostly out of a sense of duty. Now, I was being drawn into another lie. I couldn't do it.

"Samantha," I said, taking her hands again, "It's not mine."

She drew back. "But what about...?"

"I know we did," I told her. "But, you see, when I was in college I had a bad case of mumps."

She looked indignant. "What's mumps got to do with it?"

"It made me so I can't have babies." I felt as though I were explaining this to a child. For some reason, I couldn't be technical, not with her sitting there in her pedal pushers and her little white tennis shoes.

"So what're you telling me?" she asked.

I told her to call Pete. "You two did it, didn't you?" I felt like her father, or her guidance counselor. I thought of Marsha asleep in our bed, probably dreaming of babies we would never have. And Samantha, now, attributing one to me.

Samantha didn't answer. She was crying in great, heaving sobs.

"It is Pete, isn't it? If it's not me, it must be him." Damn that Pete. I wanted Samantha to answer me. Instead, she got up and left the room without another word, leaving me to stare at my watch, seeing that the hardware store was closed and that all the way home I would need to invent an excuse for Marsha as to why I, a grown man, couldn't make a toilet flush.

I finally went out to my car, and on the

windshield I thought I saw a parking ticket. It was a note from Samantha:

"I don't want him. I want you. Find a way. If you won't have me, you can't have your wife. I won't let you. I've got a gun. See you at practice. Love, Samantha.' "

Trancelike, Pete closed the diary, just as Shirley knocked.

"You OK in there?" she asked.

"Fine. I'm just fine," Pete responded in a voice an octave higher than his own. "Out in just a minute."

Then he noticed something sticky inside the back cover: a Peppermint Patty wrapper attached to an official-looking letter. Pete read it: "Jan. 16, 1968. As company commander, it is with deep personal regret that I must inform you of the missing status of Pfc. Dennis Baucom. Words cannot adequately express..."

So he *wasn't* dead, Pete said to himself.

"I'm coming in," Shirley said. She rattled the door.

"Why's this locked?" she asked.

Pete scrambled for an answer. He was a man in need of many answers.

9

– Jerry Bledsoe –
Sleep Talk

$\mathcal{A}$s he had settled to read Griffin's notebooks behind the locked bathroom door, Pete already had suspected
that this would be another sleepless night. It wasn't only
the notebooks: Shirley talked in her sleep, and whenever
she got worked up, she could go on all night long.

In the first months of their marriage, Pete had found
this intriguing and titillating. He used to lie awake, waiting
for her to start, hoping she might reveal some dark secret,
some suppressed kinkiness, but that hadn't happened.

Sometimes she shouted only a word or two. Other
times, she spewed phrases, even whole sentences. But
rarely did anything make sense. Now and then she lapsed
into grand soliloquies the equal of any Jesse Helms speech,
and just as nonsensical. But when questioned the next
morning, Shirley denied any knowledge of it.

Pete believed that nothing was without purpose, and
he thought that had to be true of Shirley's sleep talk as
well. Then one night he had been awakened by a line so
rhythmic and lyrical that he immediately realized the purpose of Shirley's subliminal recitations. She was handing
him lines for songs, a gift from another dimension. Shirley
was the vehicle chosen to deliver him his long-denied dream
— his big break in music.

After that, he kept a note pad on the nightstand and
wrote down the memorable lines as Shirley spouted them.
He was certain that it was only a matter of time before the
patterns presented themselves and a hit song emerged.

Twenty-five years earlier, when Pete had come back to country music, he had dreamed of being a star. Then, anybody with a sad enough story could make it, and heaven knew that Pete's was sadder by far than most. But alcohol had suppressed the awful memories that underlay his sadness, drowning his dreams.

Country music was different now. You had to wear big cowboy hats and leap around the way Mick Jagger had done before senility set in. You had to use laser beams and lots of fog and backup singers in skimpy dresses. A sad old guy with a battered guitar and a broken voice wasn't enough anymore, except in that book Shirley liked so much.

Yet, there were bright spots still. These new stars wore jeans so tight that they were unlikely ever to produce offspring. And not one had ever *lived* one of his own songs — they didn't even write their own stuff. Pete knew that he still could make it as a songwriter. And now heaven had handed him Shirley, an ample and endless fount of unconscious lyrics, albeit in no particular order.

After this harsh day of surprises and confrontation, Pete desperately needed sleep so that he could think clearly. But after he'd hidden the diary and calmed Shirley's suspicions and doubts, adroitly avoiding any damning explanations, she had fallen into a restless sleep and had fired up immediately, talking, as Pete's mother used to say, a mile a minute.

Pete knew it was going to be one of those Jesse Helms nights, and he slipped from bed and retreated to his recliner in the basement, where daybreak found him just beginning to doze.

Startled awake by the sound of the doorbell, he looked at the clock: 7:30 a.m. Nobody came calling at this hour. He hurried to the door to keep the bell from waking Shirley.

Two men in unbuttoned sport coats stood there, one fiftyish, the other in his 40s.

"Mr. Houser?" said the older of the two, the one with

the Grecian-Formulaed, pomaded hair.

"Yes."

"I'm Special Agent B.A. Braddock of the SBI. This is Wesley Davis, homicide investigator for the Wake County Sheriff's Department. Wonder if we might talk with you for a minute."

Somehow he wasn't surprised. Not after all that had happened in the last 36 hours. So after all these years, it finally was going to come out.

"Uh, sure," he said. "Come on in."

"Understand you knew Donald Griffin," Davis said as they seated themselves in the living room.

"Well, yes."

"How well?"

"He was my band director in high school. And after I got through college, I went back to Eastern High to teach but he'd left under some kind of cloud. Guess you heard about that." Pete thought he might have volunteered too much.

"Get out of my way!" came a shout from the bedroom, startling both detectives. Davis' hand went instinctively for the 9 mm on his left hip. Then another: "Don't you dare shut that door!"

Pete ignored it. "Would y'all like some coffee?"

The detectives declined, looking questioningly at one another as Pete went to the kitchen.

"When was the last time you saw Mr. Griffin?" Davis asked when Pete returned.

"About three years ago, I think," Pete said. "Ran into him at the Jiffy Lube. I heard he died. What is this about anyway?"

"We're looking into a few things," Braddock said.

"Ever heard of a place in Greensboro called the Lavender Garter?" Davis asked.

"No, not really," Pete said.

"Well, it was a cross-dresser bar. Burned down three years ago. We found a body there with a stocking around its neck. The body was charred so bad a positive ID was impossible. At first it was thought that he had died of a condition called autoerotic asphyxiation."

Surely he couldn't be talking about Mr. Griffin, Pete thought. *He didn't even like cars.*

"It's a game some men play," Davis went on.. But a few carry it a little too far and end up hanging themselves."

"Whap it! Whap it!" came the cry from the bedroom. "Don't let it in here!"

"Is that something you need to take care of?" Braddock asked.

"It's just my wife. She talks in her sleep."

"Well," Braddock went on. "Apparently Griffin performed there. We've heard he might have gone under the stage name Gloria Obsession."

Heavens, Pete thought, *what would he find out next?* "And you mean Griffin might have been —"

"Stomp that snake!" came a sudden shout from the bedroom, so loud that it prompted Braddock to leap to his feet, eyes anxiously scanning the floor.

Pete looked at the detectives with a helpless shrug.

"We're not sure what to think," Braddock said.

Davis rose as if eager to get going and handed him a card. "If you should come across anything that might help us, I'd sure appreciate a call."

The cache in the trunk of the Pinto flashed through Pete's mind, but it was crowded out by a phrase that resonated in his head. Stomp that snake! He could see line dancers pounding their cowboy-booted heels to it all across America.

As soon as he'd closed the door behind the detectives, he raced down to the basement and snatched up his guitar. It was then he noticed the odd clump in the trash can.

Pantyhose. And not jumbo queens either. Clearly not Shirley's. And what were these dark stains on them? Strange.

10
– Margaret Maron –
Clues

Autoerotic asphyxiation? Arson?

Absently twisting the pantyhose in his hands, Pete thought about what those homicide detectives had told him.

Solitary sex games? Cross-dressing? It seemed so out of character, yet how much did he really know about old Griffin since he was quietly forced out of Eastern High and then stopped teaching altogether? Or even before, for that matter?

Sighing, Pete dropped the pantyhose back into the trash can, stretched out again on the recliner, and picked up his guitar. He was no longer in the mood to write about stomping snakes. Instead, he strummed softly and the words wrapped themselves effortlessly around the chords.

> "Sometimes
> "These late-night times
> "Make me feel so all alone —
> "Tell me how the years have flown
> "Make me miss the friends I've known —
> "In my lifetime."

The notes faded into silence, then silence fled as his snores bounced off the concrete walls and bounded up the basement steps to the open door where Shirley stood in barefooted puzzlement. She gently closed the door and padded across the chilly kitchen tiles for a cup of the still-warm coffee Pete had made for those law officers. A ray of pale November sunshine glinted on the cut-glass sugar bowl.

She had awakened from troubled snake-filled dreams to hear strange voices in the living room, and something in their tones had kept her from letting Pete know she was awake and hearing every word.

Cross-dressing? Autoerotic asphyxiation?

Shirley wrinkled her nose in distaste. She knew exactly what the term meant because she was a guidance counselor, fully certified by Ohio and North Carolina, too. You don't get that kind of certification without enough credits in post-Freudian psychology to write a paper on abnormal sexual practices.

She glanced at the clock and moaned. Nearly 9 o'clock. She was missing CAW's breakfast session — "Signifying Crumbs: Developing Character Through Idiosyncratic Table Manners"; and if she didn't hurry, she was also going to miss "With Malice Aforethought: How to Murder for Money." Not that she could ever stoop to write in such a commercial genre, but the blurb for that session claimed that if Jane Austen were writing today, it would probably be novels of crime and detection since this was the only modern form to combine a structured plot with a comedy of manners. Shirley knew her plots could use a little structure, and mysteries were fun if not exactly comedy. The first night she dated Pete she'd gone to that Halloween party dressed as Miss Marple.

Smiling, Shirley quickly dressed, gathered up her notebook and purse and then fished around under the living room couch for the shoes she'd kicked off there while she and Pete were making up. Her fingers touched cold metal.

The gun!

Oh, gosh. How could she be thinking Miss Marple when she'd acted like Barbara Stager and almost put a bullet through Pete last night?

She put on her shoes and gingerly carried the gun with her out to the Pinto. She didn't want it in the house another minute. After dumping her purse and notebook on the front seat of the car, she unlocked the trunk and looked for some place to deposit the gun. The tarp. She could wrap it in that, except that there seemed to be something —

The briefcase tumbled from the stiff folds of the tarp, spilling spiral notebooks, blue tassels and peppermint wrappers all over her trunk.

What was so darned compelling about these notebooks that Pete would deceive her like this? She opened to a random passage dated 30 years earlier and read:

> Our two adopted daughters give us more pleasure than I ever thought possible — Motherhood has transformed Marsha into the sweet lovely girl I first married. I keep looking for their father's features as they grow older, but so far only their mother's eyes look back at me.

Shirley dropped the notebook and slammed down the trunk lid. Pete the biological father of Griffin's daughters? It couldn't be, she told herself as she started the car and headed for Chapel Hill. He'd sworn last night that the only thing he'd ever gotten from Samantha was a Peppermint Patty and in the year they'd been married, he'd never lied to her before. Or been caught at it.

And why had law officers come to their house to question him? How'd they get Pete's name?

If ever she needed a short course in deductive logic, it was now, and she skidded into an empty seat near the back of the mystery writing class only minutes after it started.

To her disappointment, the teacher wasn't the best-selling hard-boned, brass-knuckles practitioner listed in the catalog but a middle-aged woman who looked like everybody's mother.

"Where's Mike Shovel?" Shirley whispered to the beautiful young woman taking notes beside her.

"Missed his plane connection in Chicago," the young woman whispered back.

"So who's that?"

The younger woman shrugged. "I didn't catch her name, but they said one of her books won an Edgar, whatever that is."

At the front of the room, the soft-voiced matron was saying, "So if it's a question of whether the pimp was murdered by Colombian drug lords or the Mafia, my response is, 'Who cares?' It's all too random. I don't know any drug lords or Mafiosi, and dead pimps are road kill as far as I'm concerned. What interests me are domestic situations I can relate to: Is the high school principal embezzling from the building fund so that he can take the preacher's wife to Atlantic Beach for the weekend? Did old Mrs. Gotrocks die of natural causes or did one of her heirs help her along with a double dose of her heart pills? The lovely young cheerleader was pregnant when her car 'accidentally' ran off the road."

Her attention galvanized, Shirley listened as the teacher smiled and asked them, "Was it really an accident or a convenient way out of a paternity suit? And whose child was it?"

Not Pete's, Shirley told herself as the teacher read them the opening pages of a short story and began to dissect it for planted clues.

"Try to guess why I wrote this description of the husband," she said and read: "When he got out of the car, his gray slacks and blue sports shirt were drenched with perspiration and clung to his body, revealing a slight bulge at the beltline. Except for that sign of middle age, he carried himself with military precision."

"You're showing that he's starting to let himself go?" suggested the young woman next to Shirley.

"No."

"The pot belly indicates self-indulgence," said someone at the front.

"No."

Shirley raised her hand. "You want us to think his pot belly is important, but really it's the fact that he's sweating so hard that's important?"

"Bingo!" the teacher said, beaming. "That's a major clue, but it slides right by most readers because they're too busy looking at his tummy to wonder why he's sweating like a pig."

Over the next hour, she gave a dozen more examples of how to plant clues, and each time Shirley came up with the right solution.

As the class ended, the teacher said, "I hope you're working on a mystery now because you have a nicely devious sense of logic, Ms. —?

"Graves," said Shirley. "Shirley Graves-Loggins."

"Shirley Graves-Loggins?" asked the beautiful young woman beside her. "We've been looking all over for you. I'm Andi Griffin."

From behind them came a second voice. "And I'm Mandi Griffin."

"Griffin?" exclaimed Shirley. She turned and saw her classmate's identical twin. The young woman reached into her pocket and brought out a slip of pink paper imprinted with kittens and rainbows.

Shirley recognized one of her own personalized UCB checks.

"You bought a briefcase at a garage sale," said Mandi Griffin. "It wasn't supposed to be sold, and we'd really like to have it back."

11

– Philip Gerard –
Sam Mobutu

"I paid good money for it!" Shirley said.

"Well, there's been a misunderstanding," said one of the girls, just as flaming haired Monica raced by and grabbed Shirley by the elbow, "You can't miss this session, Shirl. Time to wake up and smell the cappucino. This one will jump start your life."

Shirley's life was feeling plenty jump-started right now. She turned to the girls, and yelled through the classroom door, "I'll meet you in the lounge after this. In half an hour."

They were already late.

"Imagine a girl who has three lovers," Sam Mobutu was whispering to the all-woman class in a voice full of sex and promise. "Imagine two boys and a man, all in love with a girl who doesn't even know who she is yet."

Shirley checked her CAW schedule one more time to make sure she hadn't mistakenly wandered into "Steaming Up the Windows and Turning Down the Sheets: Breaking into the Romance Field." No — this was the right room: "Turning Your Life Story into a Spiritual Story Life Instructor Sam Mobutu."

Shirley had expected a mystical African shaman. She had expected the reclusive, elusive author of *Tar Heel Kitabu* and *Down and Out in Nairobi and Winston*, whose photo never appeared on dust jackets. An expatriate rumored to hang out with movie stars like Dennis Hopper and Julia Roberts down in Wilmington.

She had also expected a man.

But at the front of the room stood a tall white woman with a cloud of wild platinum hair. Middle-aged, but sexy and comfortable with her body, the kind of woman who would try anything — the kind of woman all the husbands drooled over at parties and fantasized about later while they fumbled with their wives' brassieres.

She wore a long pied robe, which Shirley recognized from "National Geographic Explorer" as vaguely Nigerian, and as she moved to and fro across the front of the class, her feet invisible, she seemed to float, a creature of air, all grace and voluptuous curves, the atmosphere of the room swishing out of her way and then filling in behind.

Sam went on in a husky voice affecting a reggae accent. "A dumb blonde majorette falls in love with her music teacher, gets pregnant. An old story, right?"

Music teacher? Pregnant majorette? Now Shirley couldn't look away from Sam Mobutu — whose blue eyes were wide with storytelling, her hands, mugless now, fluttering about in the air drawing the shape of the story.

"After the birth, she caroms from one wacky thing to another — vegetarianism, crystals, evangelical Republicanism. She starts going to caucuses, meetings, lectures — anytime an oppressed person speaks in public, she's there. Doesn't even know why."

"She's got to get in touch with her *anger*," Monica shouted.

Here we go, Shirley thought — more of her blathering patriarchal oppression stuff.

"She attends a lecture on South African apartheid at Stagville Plantation, and there she bumps into the coolest black dude you ever saw, a Nelson Mandela-meets-Denzel Washington-meets-Spike Lee kind of guy."

Some of the women looked puzzled. "Famous black men," Sam explained, and they wrote that down. "'Who are you?' he asks, and she's stuck for an answer. All along, she's been searching for the spirit woman inside. She's never been who she is. She doesn't know."

Shirley didn't know, either.

"He leads her down to the old slave quarters and helps her find out.

"Honey, she finds a spirit woman with an *attitude*."

"That's so romantic," sighed a woman on the third row.

"Right. True love. A good man. Tobe Mobutu. A man who would have stood by her forever. Gentle, smart, didn't put up with any crap from anybody, taught politics over at N.C. Central. They get married and live happily ever after for —" she hiked her billowing sleeve and consulted a giant Mickey Mouse watch —"21 years, 46 days, seven hours and 14 minutes."

"Samantha Lambert, aka 'Peppermint Patty,' became Sam Mobutu." She paused dramatically, then in a motion like a marionette she lifted herself off her feet backward and settled on the table. "Never happen, right?"

"Can we meet this paragon?" Monica said.

"At this very moment he is on a famine relief mission in West Africa — practicing what he preaches."

The class all applauded. Except Shirley.

Shirley spoke up. "Back then, before you found your spirit woman, you said there were three — two boys and a man."

"Very perceptive," Sam Mobutu said. "The boys in the band. She was sweet for a milquetoast clarinet player."

Shirley felt her stomach flutter. Pete?

Sam Mobutu rolled her big eyes to the ceiling, as if remembering lost love. "Boy was always smacking his lips for Peppermint Patty."

Shirley tried to imagine it — Pete thrashing around with this platinum she-wolf — and the picture made her feel old and tired.

"But that was in another life. From my new spirit life, I can look back and tell it like a story that happened to somebody else, somebody young and foolish. You have to go inside yourself to come out of yourself."

They all wrote that down, except Shirley.

"Like childbirth," one of the women said, and they mmm'ed and wrote that down, too.

"Everybody's life is improbable," Sam said. "What are the odds? The people we live with are strangers — they waltz into our lives trailing their own life story, full of secrets. Every life story has a secret worth telling — if you're willing to take the chance."

Shirley gripped her chair with both hands. One day you wander into a garage sale, and your whole life is different. Your husband's past comes back in a briefcase sealed with duct tape. It was like some perverted fairy tale, everything on the line now and no guarantee of a happy ending.

"People, our lives are messy. As my mentor used to say, real life is mostly hope and chance, and you don't roll many sevens."

They all wrote that down, except for Shirley.

"It ain't enough that it really happened, people. You gotta make it *seem* like it really happened. Your life story ain't a story until you turn yourself into a character. Which means finding out who lives inside you."

They all nodded and murmured assent and wrote that down. Except Shirley.

"What happened to the clarinet player?" asked a woman in a green silk pantsuit.

Shirley thought she was going to be sick.

Samantha Lambert Mobutu laughed and showed off her white flawless teeth, her pink tongue clucking like a little clam. "That sweet little nerd? Who knows. Probably settled down with a nice fat local girl, a big-haired biscuit-dipper who chain-smokes Virginia Slims, drives a Pinto, calls him 'Shug' and pumps his arteries full of fried okra and pork sausage."

Everybody laughed except Shirley. She sucked in her stomach as hard as she could and felt her face and neck burning and wished she had run that damned Pinto

into that chiropractic billboard when she'd had the chance. She patted down her hair.

"And the band teacher?"

Samantha Mobutu stopped smiling. She put a hand on her stomach, absently. "I think we're out of time," she said softly.

The women put away their notebooks and filed toward the door. When it opened, there was Pete, mouth agape, blocking the exit.

Samantha Mobutu turned and threw up her hands. "Good Lord — it's fat boy!" She pushed past the other women and grabbed him, spun him around and kissed him full on the mouth.

Even from the last row, Shirley could tell he was enjoying it far too much. She turned her back till they both were gone, then steamed out the door, down the hall, and out the building, heading for the rendezvous with the Griffins, filled with premium grade spirit woman fuel.

12
– Marianne Gingher –
Hospital Visit

At the exact moment that Samantha Lambert Mobutu enveloped him in her caftan and suctioned her mouth to his, 27 years scrolled backward for Pete to the last time they had kissed. Samantha had lain clinging to life in her Rex Hospital bed. "If you'll live, I'll marry you," he promised, smitten by the docile and abandoned-looking sight of her.

Her eyes fluttered and her lips moved. Pete could scarcely hear her. "I'll marry you," he repeated boldly.

Fool that he was, he wished it were possible that the baby was his. But although he'd bragged stuff to the guys in the high school locker room, Pete's idea of a dream date was with a pig's foot and a bottle of beer, and maybe a little making out afterward. He felt certain that the baby wasn't Denny's — but maybe he was wrong. Denny used to get this Pat Boone gleam in his eyes and claim that he was saving Samantha for marriage. He'd confided to Pete that his biggest regret about going to Vietnam was that he was still a virgin, and Denny's parents both preached at the Righteous Snake Tabernacle of Judgment and Redemption down the road near Fuquay — he wouldn't lie, would he?

By the time Pete sat and tried to make sense of her cryptic conversation, he'd already confronted Griffin on the matter and had the band director's blood on his hands as well.

Weeks before Samantha's gun went off, Pete had demanded that Griffin meet him in the meadow down by the Haw. Pete knew of Sam's pregnancy and naturally suspected Griffin. He'd watched him with her one night at the Stallion Club in Durham, when Pete and Denny had played backup for a new group from Nashville, and learned something about how to move to a slow rhythm. Something was going on.

"You owe it to Sam to own up to this!" Pete started off.

"This is none of your beeswax, kid, and besides, there's no way the baby could be mine."

"Why not?"

"Mumps," Griffin said morosely. "I had them when I was younger, and they defused me."

"Oh, right," Pete said sarcastically, looking down at his Weejuns, then right up into Griffin's eye. "However, you could be lying, sir."

"And you, son, might find it convenient to shift the blame to some other guy."

"Why would I want to do that? I love Samantha," Pete blurted.

"You do?" Donald Griffin looked like a man facing a firing squad that was suddenly out of bullets.

"In a manner of speaking, I —" Pete stammered.

"Does Denny know?"

"Does Denny know what?"

"That you love the girl he intends to marry?"

"Does Denny know that you and Samantha —"

"You have no proof!" Griffin seethed. "And no one will take her little majorette's word against the band director's!"

That's when Pete hauled off and socked him. Griffin's hypocrisy both sickened and angered Pete.

They traded punches until they were both worn out. "Denny can't be the father!" Pete yelled, swinging a last weary jab. "Because I want to be and you ought to be and Denny's a dad-blame virgin!"

"Ha!" Griffin shouted, dodging Pete's fist. "One and

one do not always equal two in Christian arithmetic."

"You know how we've had to keep his jazz band secret from his parents. The boy is a genuine pearl. Do you think Samantha would have fun with a guy who made her pray for God's forgiveness every time she suggested getting into the back seat?"

Mr. Griffin wiped his bloody nose on his sleeve and shrugged.

"What if Denny could see us now?" Pete lamented. "I feel so ashamed."

They stopped fighting. All they could hear was the sloshing tympani of the Haw River.

"If his folks hear of this..." Pete said. "You've got to swear that Denny's out of this. Swear!"

Six months later, when news of Denny's death reached town, Sam ran directly down to the Haw with her gun in a picnic hamper, took wobbly aim at her troubled heart, and shot.

"If you'll live, I'll make an honest woman of you," Pete told her the next day at the hospital.

"I'm already honest," she croaked.

"It's just an expression. It means —"

"Silly boy, I know what it means." She laid a pale hand on his own. Her wrists were as thin as drummer's sticks. "Thanks for the gentlemanly offer, but I can't marry you because you don't love me...enough. How's that for honesty?"

Her blunt dismissal made him feel inept as well as bereft.

"I beat him up for you," Pete blustered.

"Beat who up?"

"Donald Griffin. He should 'fess up to what he did and start looking after you."

"Oh, Pete. Don't judge him too harshly. There are things you don't know."

"Who do you love?" Pete asked gently.

"The father of this baby," she said softly. There were tears in her eyes. "Do you think I could marry a boy who cleaned his ears with his finger?"

"Oh. Sorry." Pete took his finger out of his ear.

"By the same token, could I marry a boy who was a virgin? Of course, some boys lie about such things."

"They do?"

She mockingly rolled her eyes at him. She'd lain in a coma, and now she was talking and looking frisky. It was a turning point, and Pete knew he should ring for Nurse Clydesdale. "Do you really think that Denny is dead?" she said out of the blue. "Couldn't it have been a mistake?"

Pete leaned closer still and kissed her.

"I'm a basically positive and optimistic person," she said. "Like Denny."

With that remark, she faded, and try as he might, Pete couldn't rouse her. On his drive home, Pete thought a lot about Denny. If Denny was the father, it was better that he had been killed clean in Vietnam than to return home and face exposure of his sin by the Righteous Snake Tabernacle. His parents would take over where the Vietcong had left off — no joke.

"Dad disappeared three years ago," said Andi Griffin. She and Mandi and Shirley were sitting at the satellite bar, and the Griffins had been telling their story. "Our mother told us last year that we're adopted, and that Dad had always been odd about the subject, really sensitive. Of course we were furious to learn so late."

"What about your real parents?"

"Mom said it had been part of the arrangement that we would never know. Then she told us about this briefcase in the attic, and when we looked it was gone! Can you help us, Miss Graves?"

13
– Bland Simpson –
Bad Connections

*O*nly connect, she thought. Somebody at the CAW conference had said this was his advice to all aspiring writers. Now Shirley had some connecting to do.

She had holed up in a sleeper car at the Roundhouse Hotel in a railroad yard north of North Raleigh. The Roundhouse, a Lazy Susan for locomotives, had been converted into a strange and wonderful steel rail nostalgia trip. You got to eat with real railroad silver, the heavy stuff, and you didn't check into a room, you got a sleeper.

Shirley and Pete used to come out here for what they liked to call a little "all-the-way choo-choo!" but there would be no more of that for a while – Pete's little engine had gone off on the wrong trunk. Now Shirley Graves-Loggins needed to get a handle on things.

Shirley set her laptop on her berth and spilled out the haunted briefcase and a pile of documents the Griffin girls had given her. Whatever it is, she figured, it's all here — letters, notes, poems (maybe they were lyrics), and 30 or 40 envelopes of those old ripply-edged black-and-white photographs from the '60s, family pictures, band practice.

If Andi and Mandi Griffin were Donald Griffin's kids, was Samantha their mother? Was it possible they were Pete's? And if this cross-dressing business was true, did Griffin ever really have the do-wop-she-bop to be the father? And was Griffin dead or not?

She decided she'd sift through paternity before murder — that seemed like the right progression. The words of

Sherlock Holmes rang in her mind: Eliminate every possibility, and whatever remains at the end, however implausible, is the solution.

Shirley remembered the card that Detective Braddock had left behind a few days before, and pulled it from her purse:

```
BRAD BRADDOCK, Det.
ANTI CRIME — ON LINE— ALL THE TIME
INTERNET BradBrad@Raleighwood
PublSafe-T-I'mYourManCradleToGrave
PostNoBillsBurmaShave!
```

"I'm going surfing!" Shirley said, as if she'd done this more than twice before. Her Internet course at Wake Tech and her sleuth's instincts were now her essential tools.

ENTER PASSWORD, the screen line ordered her. Using her old CB handle, she clacked in: SHIRLTHESWIRL. Bingo!

THANK YOU, SHIRLTHESWIRL, WELCOME TO USERGROUP NOVITIATE LEVEL 2. CLICK ON FIST ICON FOR ENFORCEMENT.

"I'm in, I'm IN!" Shirley laughed. then she clicked her way toward Braddock.

ENFORCER >> LOG IN

"INSPECTOR BRADDOCK," she began, talking as she typed, "THIS IS SHIRLEY GRAVES. NEED TO KNOW WHAT ALL YOU DIDN'T TELL MY HUSBAND WHEN YOU PAID US A VISIT THIS MORNING."

ENFORCER >> THANK YOU, SHIRLTHESWIRL. AFTER YOU LOG-IN, HOW 'BOUT A FLOGGIN?

Could that be Braddock? Shirley was confused. In a panic she double-clicked on GEO-? to find out where she was.

SHIRLTHESWIRL IS AT HOME IN BONDAGEGROUP, ENFORCEMENT ENVIRONMENT.

"Whoa, son!" Shirley shouted. "Shirl is not at home in that little corner, no ma'am, no sir!"

Then came two sharp knocks at the door, and a dark-skinned man with an Indian accent entered with his hand out: "Missus Graves, yes?" he asked. "I am perhaps needing a more volume deposit on your telephone?" He pointed to the computer and modem lines. "On line!" he said. "Fifty dollars please."

"Who are you?" Shirley said.

"I am Roundhouse owner!" the Indian said.

Shirley knew who the owner here was — Captain Ollie O'Shay, a retired railroad engineer who used to make the 'Palmetto' run up and down the seaboard, back when there was a Seaboard Coast Line.

"What happened to Cap'n Ollie?"

"My family and I made him an irreputable offer," the man said. "But not to worry — Captain Ollie still here. He sits nightly in our Gandy Dancer Lounge singing songs and telling stories of your Southron railways. On salary, Captain Ollie is very much a person of color. And so...fifty dollars please."

For what?

"For me not to turn off the telephone."

"The old Roundhouse'd let you pay when you checked out."

"Yes and that of course was charming. But then there was no Internet, and this is the new Roundhouse."

This was going to be an expensive weekend. Shirley found two 20s and a 10 wadded in her cosmetics bag, paid him to get rid of him, and rushed back to Detective Braddock.

Shirley, mighty curious now, returned to the ENFORCEMENT room, and noticed one of the postings: BADSIDE. This rang a terrible bell. Actually, there was a whole thread of BADSIDEs on file, and she pulled the most recent BADSIDE.3006. Suddenly the tube flipped, flopped and flew alive with squares, triangles and Greek letters, tell-tales of intercomputer skirmishing, occasional English text and then musical notes not on a staff but merely given in sequence by their letter names: F A D C F A D.

"Lost something in translation," Shirley said. She almost clicked out, but her eyes lit on the last block of text:

And then I saw you a-gin,
My thoughts unlawful as sin.

Not the lyric, but the apparently transparent crypto-gram of the musical notation appearing as letters, kept her gazing at the screen:

And then I saw you a-gin,
B E D D E D G
My thoughts unlawful as sin.
D E A D E D G

Shirley Graves nearly flipped. If BEDDED meant bedded and DEADED meant killed, and if G was Donald Griffin? Whose lyric draft was this anyhow? Just one click revealed the sender's name:
Monica Jeffers.
Monica! Her once best friend! But where on earth did that lead? No pronoun preceded the simple code, no "I" or "you" to suggest whether this was a confession or an accusation. Or was it a report from one conspirator to an-other — possibly to Pete? What kind of contest were they in on together anyway? You win, you live — you lose, you die?
She felt it even more urgent to get in touch with Braddock, and she was just about to line in his address again when — in cold type right before her eyes — there lit up the words:
BRADBRAD >> GREAT STUFF, GUYS. BRING ALL SUSPECTS TO ME. REMEMBER, THE FAMILY THAT PREYS TOGETHER, STAYS TOGETHER.
Was that Detective Braddock? Who was he talking to?
SHIRL >> BRADDOCK, SHIRLEY GRAVES HERE.

INQUIRING ABOUT THE GRIFFIN MATTER.

BRADBRAD >> HELLSBELLS, WHAT ARE YOU DOING HERE?

Shirley wrote. GOT IN AMONG THE SEX-SLAVES BY MISTAKE. MORE IMPORTANT, WHAT ARE YOU DOING HERE?

BRADBRAD >> WORKING THE BEAT, LADY. PART OF A CONTINUING INVESTIGATION. A FAMILY AFFAIR.

SHIRLEY >> I HAVE VITAL INFORMATION ON GRIFFIN'S CASE. WANT TO TRADE. YOU TELL ME ABOUT GRIFFIN'S DEATH, AND I'LL TELL YOU ABOUT HIS CHILDREN.

BRADBRAD > YOU FIRST.

Then Shirley gave him an E-mail-full about the Griffin girls' story when Braddock broke in:

BRADBRAD >> GRIFFIN'S DEATH = MAY BE REVENGE KILLING, MIZ GRAVES. REASON TO BELIEVE KILLER'LL STRIKE AGAIN SOON.

SHIRL THE SWIRL >> KILLER'S SAMANTHA?

BRADBRAD >> KILLER IS A MAN.

SHIRL >> HOW KNOW?

BRADBRAD >> STRANGULATION & ARSON= MALE M.O. FOR MURDER. YOUR HUSBAND = A SUSPECT. YOU KEEP ME POSTED ON PETE.

Right, Shirley thought. I'm kinda out of the loop on Pete, dammit.

SHIRL >> OK. WILL HOLD ONTO YR CARD.

BRADBRAD >> NO! DON'T USE CARD! FROM NOW ON, GET ME AT: FAMILYMAN@CIRCLEWAGONS.COM.

Two sharp knocks came again at the door, followed by a bloodcurdling yodel. Shirley thought the hotelier was going crazy over her Netsurfing, but she was wrong.

When she opened the door, there was Monica and, behind her, a wild-eyed snaggletoothed man wearing filthy Army fatigues and a red bandana round his head — he might have just cut loose from a Vietnam Veterans Against the War march if it were 25 years ago. For a second he stood grinning, raised a harmonica to his mouth, blew in and out three times, and with his bleeding other hand shook a fireman's ax like he was keeping time with it. With jollity he said:

"How 'bout some tunes, people? Hey, don't eat the brown acid!" Then he fell forward and would have slammed into the opposite wall had he not planted the ax in it, exclaiming as he did, "FAR OUT!"

"All aboard?!" Shirley shouted.

14
– Laura Argiri –
A Blast from the Past

Facing Monica and the man with the ax, Shirley could taste the adrenalin in her mouth, metallic.

"I'm not only getting in touch with my anger," she thought, "I...am getting...intimate with it. I'm friends with my anger. I love my anger. My anger and I...are lovers." Her anger obeyed her and stayed quiet as she tried out some prime guidance counselor moves on the maniac. ("Establishing Rapport with Demented Drug Friends: Talk that Works.")

"Monica, you trash," Shirley said amiably, as if this happened often and was a matter of mild, familiar amusement between them. "Who's your new pal here?"

"Call me Ishmael," said the Ax.

"OK, Ishmael," Shirley said. "Like your fatigues, soldier." (Please holler like that again, she thought, and bring security running.)

"He thinks you can help him," said Monica. "That's why he brought me here by brute force as a hostage, and that's why he'll cut me up in pieces and put me in the trunk of a junk car if you don't tell him what he wants to know. He's a handsome bunny, isn't he?"

"You mind your mouth," said Ax, giving Monica's arm a squeeze. "I'm looking for Samantha Mobutu."

Shirley assessed his dimensions (big), his musculature (powerful, Navy SEAL or Green Beret or serious powerlifting) and his expression (askew). Shirley thought of something she'd seen in a silly old movie about Nazis:

the Beer Hall Putsch and a young Hermann Goering, with his eyes blazing and an absurd steel helmet on his head, jumping up on a table and firing a rifle into the ceiling to silence a rowdy tavern crowd: "The National Socialist Revolution has begun!"

"Are you crazy or what?" asked the new and empowered Shirley of this large man. Submission seemed the most dangerous tactic you could use with him. But he looked her over, then sang in a well-tuned tenor a line from an old song about wind blowing. Then he enunciated, "What."

"What d'you mean, what?"

"Am I crazy or what? What. I'm definitely too crazy for either of you to snark at me and score off me. I might snap, you know, and that'll be bad. It's *always bad*. I went to Nam and shot the Cong to keep democracy safe for you and your broad butts and therapy groups and vodka tonics, and now that I am back in Carolina, what do I find? I find upper/lower-uppers, and little plastic towns. For little plastic people." He lapsed once again into a song about a Miss American Pie.

"Yeah, 1973, right?" said Shirley. "I was 17." (She thought this might play to his older brother instincts.) "Where've you been since then?"

"Wherever a soldier of fortune is needed! Which is usually where poets are opening their mouths. I collected this one coming back from something called the Semiformalist She-Wolves Alternative Session. She was roiling and streeling up to her room after the ninth margarita of the evening. Dressed like this. You know she was out for more than a good rhyme."

That was easy enough to believe; Monica was turned out sort of like Dil in *The Crying Game*. No wonder Big Crazy here had seen her; she probably glowed in the dark.

"Anyway, ever since then it's been yappity-yappity-yap," said Ax, wiping his brow. "It's almost more than a post-traumatic-shock victim can be expected to stand."

"Don't sweat it. Only .00084 percent of the population pays the slightest attention to poets," Monica advised.

"There you go again. I mean all of you nineties bleed-ing-hearts and shamanists! Chapel Hill used to be music! Rage! And a man could shoot a deer and like the Tempta-tions too. There used to be Jim Morrison. Now there's Melissa Etheridge. There used to be Ginsburg! Now there's Monica Jeffers! There used to be hash and acid, now there's Prozac and coffee."

"I had to wear a bra straight through the 60s," Monica said.

"You shut your head before I light it on fire for you," said Big Crazy. "She always tries to confuse me. Where am I? "

"You were telling us your life story?" Shirley said, in her best human services mode.

"Anyway, a year ago, I met a neat guy at a gun auc-tion in Vegas, and he's hired me to work for him. He and others. Me and my fellow vet buds are go where we please, pretty much. Fighters for hire by any righteous cause. 'Guns don't kill people, we do.' That's our motto." Shirley thought: *This man sure flickers in and out, as Anthony Hopkins did so well in movies.*

"We especially target organizations like Women Against Children, Children Against Spankings, Women & Gays & Bleeding Hearts Against Guns & Beer & Hunting Dogs. Democrats & Poets Against Indigenous Rednecks & Senator Helms & the NRA, Women & Gays & Bleeding Hearts & Democrats & Poets for National Emasculation. You pay us, we paste 'em. You name 'em, we've roughed 'em up. This started out as just a routine operation, turning up the heat on a bunch of social parasites. Me, I'm the heat."

"Yeah, I can see that," said Shirley.

"And right now we're looking for Samantha Mobutu who's affiliated with about seven of the aforementioned or-ganizations. Have you met her?"

"I've heard her speak," Shirley said, uncertain

whether to divulge more.

"Hard to get at her," said Big Crazy. "Sort of like Nelson Mandela. Married an African politico and started writing books to stir up women and make them give white guys hell. I read about it in *The Nation*. She gave Women Against Vigilantes a check for $5,000!" With that, Big Crazy threw his ax into the headboard.

"You want to see Samantha Mobutu?" Shirley asked, remembering that "Establishing Rapport with Demented Friends, Part IV" had specified, when the guns start to firing, go along to get along. "No problem. I'll take you to her door. You don't even need to cut Monica in pieces and put her into a car trunk."

It was tiring, driving at axpoint. As they approached the Carolina Inn, Big Crazy directed Shirley to the service entrance. It was the hour when the night shift personnel fade and sneak off in corners and doze, their morale particularly low. For a crisp new $20 bill, a drowsy woman doing the third shift in housekeeping found Samantha Lambert Mobutu's room number for them and told them the way to go.

"What?" said the voice of a mostly sleeping Sam behind the door.

"Security. There's a problem, ma'am," said Big Crazy as the soft shift of limbs sounded on a mattress behind the door.

Finally the door was opened, and Sam Mobutu was revealed, wearing an all-natural, virgin-to-chemicals, unbleached Sea Island cotton knit nightshirt from L.L. Bean, perfectly opaque, and $37.50 if Shirley remembered this season's price correctly. Her makeup was off, her hair was down and every whichaway like an untidy sheaf of winter wheat, and she looked her age. Yet she looked her age in the way of a fully blown rose, not a beat-up sneaker.

"Oh, my God, *you're* Sam!" shouted Ishmael.

"Denny?" shouted Sam.

Then another shape shambled out of the shadows. It was Pete.

"Shirl?" asked Pete.

Shirl went for the ax.

15

– John Welter –
Room Service

It was the best of times and it was the worst of times. It was Eastern Standard Time. "Are everyone's watches synchronized?" Denny said, closing the door behind him with his foot as he looked at his wristwatch and casually pulled out from his jacket a sawed-off machine gun and pointed it at the floor. "We used to synchronize our watches all the time in Vietnam, usually before a mission, as if — in case you were going to die — you wanted to die punctually.

Sometimes we synchronized our watches before going to the bathroom. Synchronized urination, you know. Isn't that a demonstration sport in the Olympics by now? Everything else is. But just because I'm standing here with a sawed-off machine gun doesn't mean I have Post-Traumatic Stress Syndrome. That's psycho-babble. Maybe I'm experiencing nothing more complex than a bad mood."

"No worse than *my* mood!" Shirley yelled, rushing forward to try to grab the ax from Denny. "I'll kill you, you adulterer!" Shirley screamed as she struggled furiously to pull the ax loose.

"I'm not an adulterer," Denny said, keeping the ax in his grasp with little effort. "I'm not even a fornicator. Oh, I admit I've considered virtual sex, phone sex, megaphone sex, telegraph sex, mail orders, postcards, Braille..."

"I'm not talking about you, you idiot! I'm talking about him!" Shirley yelled as she pointed at Pete and continued yanking on the ax handle. "Give me this ax!"

"It's not what you think, Shirley," Pete said, standing

81

anxiously beside Samantha as Shirley continued to squirm. Denny raised up his arm, the ax, and Shirley, all in one motion, holding Shirley several inches off the floor.

"I recommend you let go before I fling you against the wall," Denny said.

Shirley released her grip and dropped to the floor, slinking away from the threat of Denny but scowling so intensely at Pete that her anger seemed almost radioactive, as if everyone who looked at her face would require medical treatment.

Shirley pulled a gun from her purse and aimed it at Pete. "This is a .38-caliber revolver. I don't know what the .38 stands for. Possibly it represents your IQ.

"And this," Monica said, aiming a tiny pistol at Denny, "is a Walther .25 automatic. I have no idea who Walther was, but he couldn't have been very nice if someone named a gun after him."

"And this gun here," Pete said as he pulled a monstrous revolver from behind him and showed it to everyone, "is a .44 Magnum. A bullet fired from this gun has enough velocity to penetrate an engine block. Anyone have an engine block?"

"How come I'm the only one here without a gun?" Samantha said morosely.

"Here's an extra," Denny said as he handed a pistol to Samantha. "It's a 9 mm. And I must say, you people are pretty heavily armed for a bunch of whining, multicultural, New Age sissies."

For a few seconds, everyone anxiously aimed their guns at Denny, except for Denny, who seemed reluctant to aim a gun at himself.

"I think we're in a Mexican standoff," Pete said.

"Why are standoffs always Mexican?" Shirley said.

"Why couldn't we be in an Austro-Hungarian standoff?" Monica said.

"Or a Mesopotamian standoff?" Samantha said.

"Well isn't that just so politically correct of everyone...to insist that even when you point a gun at someone, you want it to be culturally diverse," Denny said.

"I don't know why you gave me this gun. I can't shoot you," Samantha said to Denny.

"You mean you still love me?" Denny said.

"No. Because I don't know how to release the safety," Samantha said, frowning at the gun, then staring with curiosity at Denny. "And besides, I've always believed that the pen is mightier than the sword."

"Then why didn't they send us to Vietnam armed with ballpoint pens?" Denny said. "Whenever we saw the Viet Cong, we could've said, 'Halt, or I'll write a troubling essay!'

"But I'm digressing," Denny said. "I'll bet you didn't know I could digress. I bet all of you self-important Chapel Hill intellectuals don't think that a mere Vietnam veteran has the acute mental sophistication required to lose track of what he's saying and ramble on pointlessly about wholly peripheral subjects, such as my old family recipe for rancid mashed potatoes with decomposing gravy."

"You always were so down-to-earth," Samantha said. "So gravitational, so earthy, so dirt-like, a man of whom you could say. 'He's covered with topsoil.' Which reminds me...I thought you were dead. We got word saying you'd been killed in action."

"I don't know why everybody but me was notified of my death," Denny said resentfully. "Oh, sure...send telegrams to everybody in the United States, but don't even bother to tell me of my own sorrowful death. It was a bureaucratic mistake. My military records were mixed up with someone else's. When I found out I was regarded as dead, I just walked away from the war."

"You simply walked away?" Pete said.

"I didn't have a car," Denny said.

Samantha stepped closer to Denny and said, "Oh,

Denny. If only I'd known."

"Well even if you'd known, the expense of sending a car to Vietnam is astronomical," Denny said. "There's shipping fees, insurance, import duties, bribes..."

"No, Denny. I mean if only I'd known you were still alive, then...then...then..."

Denny reached his hand toward Samantha and said gently: "Perhaps you should start a different sentence; one you can finish."

"But what have you been doing all these years?" Monica said, "And more to the point, why did you come here with a machine gun, a pistol and an ax?"

"Well, originally, I was going to hold everyone hostage," Denny said. "And I'd still do it if everyone would put their guns down."

Everyone shook their heads no.

"But let me explain," Denny said, sitting on the bed, where Samantha sat beside him. "As you remember, my father was a minister at the Igneous Rock Baptist Tabernacle; igneous, of course, referring to geological formations created by solidified lava during the Precambrian Era 600 million years ago during the Eisenhower Administration, I believe."

"You're digressing again," Shirley said.

"And thank you for noticing," Denny said. "Anyway, you know I come from a strict family," Denny said. Like all decent Americans, my parents believed that when love and gentleness weren't enough to raise a child right, coercion was useful. And anyway, to make a long story unbearable, I recently joined this paramilitary organization whose goal is to wipe out the national epidemic of liberals."

"So you're an antibiotic?" Pete said.

"Are you being sarcastic?" Denny said.

"Antiseptic," Monica said.

"Well, think of me as an ideological goo, if you want to," Denny said. "But I must admit, it all changed for me when my employers sent me here to abduct certain local enemies...meaning you, Samantha. But as soon as I realized who you were, as soon as I remembered how beautiful you are and longed to be reunited with your lips, your bosom, you thorax, your dorsal and ventral sides, your lower extremities, the discrete curvature of your abdominal surfaces..."

"You sound like a medical examiner," Samantha said. "You can't just come back into my life after being presumed dead, after coming here to sweep me away with an ax, after discussing my qualities as if I were a dissected frog. I need time to think. I'm confused. Nothing makes sense right now."

"I blame the author," Shirley said.

"Well, if I can't have you," Denny said with a disturbed glint, "I might as well shoot something."

He abruptly stood up from the bed and wildly swung the barrel of his machine gun around the room, making everyone duck and drop to the floor.

"I'll kill the one thing in your life that matters above all else," Denny said to Samantha.

Pete began whimpering and tried to crawl under the bed as he yelled. "No! No! No!"

Denny smiled as he fired a horrifying burst of bullets.

Samantha held her face in her hands and wept. Her laptop computer was deceased. Someone kicked in the door to Samantha's room and yelled, "Police!"

"Wrong room. They're not here!" Denny shouted as he raised the window and dived outside into the subsequent chapter.

16

– Jaki Shelton Green –
Blues Song

It was a hot evening as Gloria Obsession sat facing four beveled, slanted, out-of-focus stage makeup mirrors. "I am more beautiful than a thousand Peppermint Patties."

That was how the litany began each night as Gloria Obsession looked in the lopsided mirrors of his past. He loved the smell of makeup. His nose could choose colors; barely there beige, cinnamon frost, cool melon, tango apricot. Tonight he chose translucent bronze for the hollow of his cheeks. An Aztec frosted look was what he wanted for tonight. Gloria Obsession was on his way to his debut at the Coltrane Lounge.

The Coltrane Lounge was one of the best-kept secrets in the pit of black Durham. One of Gloria's friends, stage-named Patty Cake, had taken him in after the fire at the Lavender Garter, where Gloria had entertained for years. Now that Gloria and his piano-player were back in the Triangle, after three years in Savannah, Patty Cake said it was time for a comeback...at a black club. "Show them, girl, strut your stuff tonight," Patty Cake had told him. "If you can't handle this crowd, no white woman can."

Gloria Obsession had always wanted to go in drag to the Coltrane Lounge and for just one night pretend that she was as much a woman as the black women whom she adored. She'd studied them all her life; she loved their playfulness and the simplicity and the way they moved in dresses just as tight as the dress she'd chosen tonight.

As Gloria slowly applied Earth-clay rouge to his cheekbones, Donald Griffin was already at his job at the club, sitting in a circle of yellow light, playing the chords to an old Otis Redding tune. The music took his mind back to another dark speakeasy in colored Durham 30 years ago, where he'd taken the boys to play back-up for a hot new group out of Tennessee.

The kids were amazed, terrified and wildly excited. "You mean these colored folks want us to come play behind the Righteous Cruisers. Us!?" Pete nearly peed his pants getting that last "us" out of his flaccid jaws.

"Well it's like this — we're all there is for musicians who can read sheet music in this neighborhood. Besides, I've been knowing these cats for a long time. They'll tolerate us fine. See if we can learn something." This surprised the boys, who had only known him as their proud band director. And so they all ended up in the Stallion Club, with its brand-new red vinyl and chrome chairs and velvet couches and the first strobe light the boys had ever seen and mirrors everywhere.

Griffin and two scared-to-death red-faced little snots arrived to face an already gloriously inebriated crowd of older black folks who seemed not to notice that they were white or to care if these "grinning too much" little white boys were trying to impress them with their learned syncopation. After all, the main attraction was the baddest black jukebox group on the East Coast. What did anyone care about the local white boys sitting behind them? The boys and I actually played good, he thought to himself. Yeah, we played good enough for the prettiest colored woman in the room to get up and slow dance against the wall by the bandstand.

Poor Baucom stood sweating buckets of water onto his sneakers and watched every movement the lovely caramel faun choreographed as if the wall were Otis Redding, inviting her dips and swoons and bends of hips.

That was the same night, Griffin remembered, as he

picked up a much too weak gin and tonic, that Little Miss Peppermint Patty decided that "she wanted to taste," as she put it, what Mrs. Griffin "continued to waste." It was 1:30 in the morning. He'd dropped both boys home, sat in the car, watched porch lights blink on, then off. "Thanks again, Mr. Griffin, good night." He headed home the long way, cutting through Al Perkins' land to see the lake eyeballing a restless sky. Even full-moon-bodied clouds seemed to gather in large configurations suggesting a cold snap.

I was tired — he said to himself, as if confessing — sleepy, trying to focus on the road ahead of me through dust that was forming strange patterns in the headlights. When out of nowhere the bicycle appeared in front of me. Samantha! It was Samantha in pale blue baby-doll pajamas. Hair waving like snow because of all the dust covering the windows. I slammed on the brakes just as she swerved to the left, scratching the paint on the "family" car.

"Oh, it's you," Griffin sighed.

"Of course, it's me," said a grinning Samantha. "Can I get in? I've just got a flat."

We put her bike in the trunk. As soon as she opened the door the inside light spotlighted the blond fuzz on her legs. I'd seen this fuzz before, and it always drove me crazy. This time I did not look away. Head spinning, my hands were no longer driving the car but simply making small circles of O's all over her thighs.

"I guess I'm a woman now — more woman than that woman you married who does nothing but drive this stupid car back and forth to the grocery store," a red-faced Samantha cooed a few minutes later as she stepped away from the car. It seemed so long ago, Griffin thought as he beckoned for another drink.

A sultry, dark, moaning, blues woman held the air in her throat, bellowing out throaty words as Gloria Obsession slithered into the small narrow door of the Coltrane Lounge. Her $35 luxurious human hair sable lashes shadowed eyes which she had dusted with kohl liner and her favorite midnight blue glaze. Gloria knew she had every eye — of every woman in the joint. The emerald green plunging-neckline-slit-up-the-back dress sculpted over her Playtex padded hips screamed at these women to "Take notice, because I am here!"

Now it was Gloria's turn.. She picked up the mike and started to sing under the dusty yellow spotlight:

"Baby, you moved like a razor
Cut me to the bone
Sent me to the graveyard
But I'm not goin' alone.
We'll go together, baby,
to that place in the dark
and dig, dig, dig
till all those secrets fly.
We'll go together baby,
but I'll wave bye-bye."

The sound of his best friend's voice made Griffin almost choke on his own breath as he played the minor blues chords. The music was suddenly too loud, too revealing, too sad, as Griffin recalled all that he had lost. His marriage, on the skids long ago, finally suffocating. Then his twin daughters, would he ever be able to tell them the truth? And finally, the lost love behind it all.

After her set, Miss Gloria Obsession headed for the bar. By 2:30 a.m. she'd finished her fourth peppermint schnapps cocktail. She then pulled out her rhinestone heart-shaped mirror to check her damp, frizzing and fopping French twist. Just as she pursed her lips for the lipstick, a much too rough Special Agent Braddock pushed his knee into her Playtex padded hips and twisted her free hand into a pair of handcuffs. "Drop the lipstick, honey. You're under arrest."

A teary-eyed, half-drunk Donald Griffin saw what was

happening and shouted: "Get your dirty cop hands off her!"
By the time he staggered from his piano seat, two other
cops had pinned him down on a nearby bar stool, hand-
cuffed him and dragged him out the door along with Gloria
Obsession and several other cross-dressers and prostitutes.
The patrol car turned on its blue light and sped away.

17
Michael Chitwood
Getting religion in RTP

*T*he unmarked car carrying Pete, Shirley, Samantha and Monica slowed as it took a right off Interstate 40 onto Davis Drive and rolled into Phase II of Research Triangle Park. The landscape quickly turned from modern buildings to pines and broom sedge. Here future eggheads and geeks would one day work on the gene that causes people to isolate genes. The car passed several scraped and raw-looking construction sites, then pulled behind a patrol car. Gloria Obsession, three prostitutes and Donald Griffin stood by another blue-suited officer.

"This is the Research Triangle Park," Shirley said, clutching the briefcase and her laptop. "North Carolina's crown jewel of science."

"You people get moving," said the officer. Griffin remembered bellowing through a megaphone at lagging band members. "You all ready for a new life? Ready or not, follow me."

"I've already had more lives than a striped cat," Samantha said to herself. Shirley stumbled in the rough road, and Pete caught her around her ample waist. Their eyes met. For the first time since this whole thing began, neither looked away.

"Two roads diverged in a yellow wood," Monica thought. Gloria billowed. She looked like a mica-spangled dust cloud being driven before storm winds. And Griffin brought up the rear.

"Keep moving people," said the officer.

Just out of sight of the road, the crowd came upon a sort of lean-to. Three walls and a roof had been fashioned from pine boughs, and over a makeshift archway was scrawled in white paint: "The Family That Preys Together." The "e" in "preys" faced the wrong way. "A brush arbor," Pete whispered. "Haven't seen one of those since I went with Grandma to services in Siler City."

"Find a seat," the officer hissed. As the feet of the metal folding chairs sank into the thick needles, who should appear on a small stage but Special Agent Braddock?

"Twenty-five years as a special agent," Braddock began, peeling off his battered topcoat to reveal a white suit, a red, white and blue tie, and an Old Glory lapel pin. "Twenty-five years and I've seen it all. Murder. Rape. Incest. Drugs. And after all those years, with liberals spending more on crime every year, has it gotten better?"

Pete looked around to see if anyone was going to answer.

"No," said Braddock.

"And now you people," Braddock continued. "Technically, there's nothing to charge you with…except the crime of moral decay. Assaulting decency. Assaulting the family."

"Well, our family's seen better days," Shirley had to admit to herself.

"But I've brought you here to give you a chance. Five years ago, like-minded individuals met at a weapons show in Las Vegas and united behind the three G's — God, Guns and Getting the government off our backs. From that meeting, The Family was born. The Family is now ready for a second generation. It's ready for you."

"Wait till The Family gets a load of me," Gloria Obsession whispered. A guard reached for his gun. There was silence.

Underbrush at the side of the arbor rustled as a solitary figure, with ammo belts crossing his bare chest, rolled into a nearby ditch.

Braddock paused — looked to one side — then put

his hands together prayerfully. "There was once a small town where children were safe to play on the sidewalks. Neighbor spoke to neighbor. People went to bed at night with their doors unlocked. Everybody was happy. NOBODY tried on each other's clothes."

" BOMC crap," Monica thought.

"Who is this Macy's balloon talking to?" Gloria whispered to Sam. Braddock now looked inflated inside his white suit.

"Ladies and gentlemen, you are now on ground zero of the next American Revolution. This will be a revolution for real Americans — God-fearing couples with 2.3 children. Heterosexual, of course. That's right, I'm talking about families, families with values. Ladies and gentlemen, you are now on the site of the Center for the Study of American Values, the Death Penalty and the Social Importance of the Assault Rifle. This think tank for God is the newest tenant of North Carolina's crown jewel, the Research Triangle Park.

"Told you it was the crown jewel," Shirley cooed to Pete.

"Not a penny for the capital campaign will come from taxpayers'," Braddock went on, "and that's where you come in. We need you to show how mired in the mud we've gotten. Your sordid stories — teenage lust, affairs, illegitimacy and fondness for soppy novels — are the fodder we need for our fund-raising effort. Oprah won't be able to resist. But first, you've got to believe."

He punched the button on a boom box, and organ music began.

"Now what I need from you, brothers and sisters, is for you to come home, to be welcomed back into the bosom, the great maternal bosom, of the Family. Won't you come home now? Home to God. Home to guns. Home to gracious living."

"Hey, it's 'Where better living begins,'" Shirley shouted. "That's Cary you're talking about."

"Now sing with me now, in the words of that great old hymn: Just as I am without one plea."

Gloria had heard enough.

"Tell it. Yes, tell it," she began to shout as the others started feebly to sing along.

Braddock and the officers looked uneasy. They liked nice, quiet, well-behaved revivals.

Then Pete stood, raised both hands and began to wave them over his head. He moaned in an unknown tongue. Monica remembered she still had a king snake from the CAW conference in her purse. "Thou shalt take up serpents," she shouted and draped the sleepy snake around her neck and marched toward Braddock.

Pete whispered to Shirley, "You're a recovering fundamentalist, for Christ's sake, get with the program!"

From the brush, Denny "Big Crazy" Baucom readied his AK-47. The tanks he had in mind weren't for thinking.

18

– Clyde Edgerton –
Reunion at the Governors Inn

Night owls cocked their heads. "Just as I am?" Frogs — now silent — listened. One thousand feet up, Hortense the nighthawk circled lazily and watched below as human beings danced around a brush arbor in the bright light of automobile headlights. Hortense wondered if she were viewing a parade, a paradox, a parable, a parody, perhaps a metaphor, a message or a re-enactment like on "Rescue 911."

Special Agent Braddock was first surprised and then pleased that the revival was going so well; he believed he was in true fact witnessing the Family Values Revival of America. He and his followers were on the brink of cleansing the dirt of confusion from the face of America. If these degenerate-fiction-writer-poet-musician-transvestite-homosexual-vegetarian-dope smoking-cross-dressing liberals could be struck with the spirit of his God, Guns and Getting Rid of Government movement, so could all other lesser sinners.

The rousing rendition of "Just As I Am" broke into "Just A Closer Walk With Thee." Denny, in the underbrush, could take it no more. First, it was seeing again Samantha's beauty and remembering the precious breath of innocent first love. Then, the sight of the king snake and the brush arbor with the unfolded folding chairs. He was swept back into his mama and daddy's little church in Fuquay. He remembered, as if struck by lightning, the kind old folks from that church who had loved him as a son. He remembered dinner on the grounds, the smell of hymnbooks and saw-dust, he remembered the words of Jesus, "Do unto others as you would have them do unto you." He remembered compassion, he remembered music. He had over the years somehow come to believe that his fundamentalist past was a program for pride and power, vengeance and violence, yet through memory he was finding, folded softly in the wings of fundamentalism, a human heart of tolerance.

"Just A Closer Walk With Thee" broke into "Coming In On a Wing and a Prayer," which broke into "Praise God and Pass the Ammunition." Denny snapped. Yes, snapping from The Family's intolerance and dark hatred into a rev-elation of bright peace and justice, he rose from the weeds, leaped into the clearing and opened fire, tracing a pattern of bullets into the sky and shouting: "Samantha, I'm back. I'm tan, rested, tested and ready. Braddock, you and your fruitcakes reach for the sky. The rest of you head for cover. This could get nasty."

Pete and Shirley held hands as they ran through the dark woods.

"Where are we going?" Pete asked.

"For help," Shirley said.

"Right," Pete said.

They had run only a few yards when they saw a lonely reporter with a flashlight and a computer disk under his arm coming straight at them with steel-hard determina-tion on his face.

"Is Braddock over there?" he asked.

"Who are you?" Shirley asked.

"Pat Stitch. Just doing my job, ma'am. We're going to expose Braddock for, among other devious schemes, enticing highway patrolmen to work on off-duty hours in public schools as teachers' aides for cash. We've got it all documented, right here." He waved the disk at her.

Hortense, high above, saw helicopters and Civil Air

Patrol spotter planes rise in the night from the staging area at The Deli on N.C. 54.

Stitch continued: "Braddock has confused God with Guns and Guns with Guts, and dress and sexual delight with the Devil, and the Bible with the Constitution, and the Constitution with the Devil, and the devil with the blue dress on."

"It's darn confusing," Pete said.

"But we'll get him," Stitch said. And off he marched, looking at the choppers in the sky and at his watch.

Up on I-40, Pete and Shirley walked along the shoulder. "Let's just walk on to the Governors Inn," Pete said. Just then a battered pickup slowed and pulled over, apparently to offer them a ride.

"Should we?" asked Shirley.

"Yes," said Pete. "Look. There's a guitar on the gun rack. I'll get our bags. You get the briefcase."

The driver was a little dried-up fellow wearing a turtleneck and a gray hair weave. "Hop in," he said. "The road is a way of life, and certain roads come but once in a lifetime."

Shirley recognized the driver, punched Pete, and then said loudly, " BOMC."

"Book-of-the-Month Club?" reflexed the driver.

"No, *Bridges of Madison County*. Aren't you Robert James Waller?!"

"You must be one of my fans. Where to?"

"The Governors Inn. Just down the road. I need some rest," said Pete.

"The weary come and the weary go. Thus but once in a lifetime do the weary truly find rest."

"Oh, Pete, couldn't we have one little drink with Jimmy?"

"I never drink with a man wearing hair spray," said Pete.

"Actually, I only drink with lonely women whose husbands are at the state fair with their cows. That's why I'm in North Carolina. State Fair. And I don't believe in family values, by the way."

"That's a load off my mind," said Pete.

"The state fair's over," said Shirley.

"Over where?" asked Waller.

Suddenly, the old pickup coughed, stuttered and was silent. Waller guided it to the roadside. "These old pickups are so sentimental. Engine trouble like this comes but once in a lifetime."

"Let's go, Pete," said Shirley. "I'm with you, big boy. He talks funny."

"Have you got the briefcase?" asked Pete.

"Yes. It's right here."

As they trudged into view of the Governors Inn entrance, Shirley read aloud from two spotlighted banners:

"WELCOME: W.E.E.P. SONGWRITING AWARDS DINNER

WELCOME: CAW CLOSING SESSION DINNER"

Pete and Shirley stood staring at each other. "I can't believe we forgot," said Shirley.

On the lawn two men were digging with shovels.

"Aren't you Tim McLaurin?" said Shirley. "What are y'all doing?"

"Yes ma'am, I am Tim McLaurin, and this is Clyde Edgerton, aka Sky King. Oh, I've learned 'bout all I can 'bout snakes. So Sky and I are into fishing worms now. They don't bite. Out here in this lawn of purple sage fescue we find the basic red wriggler. Cute little rascal. Excuse me, but me and Sky got to get back to diggin'."

In the lobby, Pete and Shirley read on the announcements board that the Songwriter's Contest dinner was being held in the main dining room and that the CAW closing session dinner was being held in the Edmisten Memorial

Yard Care Room.

As Pete and Shirley entered the main dining room, Dave "The Caveman" Pickins announced the winning song was "Bring Your Bad Side to the Bed Side."

Pete was overcome. Shirley was proud.

"Let's check in," said Shirley, "shower, and then come back down."

"Yes. Yes," said Pete. "The night is but a puppy dog."

Once in their room, 211, Pete and Shirley collapsed onto the bed. "I'm exhausted," said Pete.

"Bed!" exclaimed Shirley. "On the bed! In the Round-house I'd just spread Griffin's notebooks, and was about to read — hold on, listen to this." Shirley opened the brief-case, thumbed through the notebooks, and found this page:

> July 17, 1967
>
> Back from the band room. She has confessed all. Now I know. It wasn't me. It was Denny. And Denny was the one she loved, probably happened the night he left for Nam. She can't tell him — his parents will disown him, and she's not sure how he'll take it either. She's distraught. I finally thought of a way out: I'd take the baby. She's too young to raise it, and I won't have her thinking of anything else. She's graduating. Wants to travel in Africa. We've wanted kids, Marsha and I, and we'll adopt it, if Samantha keeps it quiet. She wants Denny more than anything else, and I just pray he makes it out.

"So that was it," said Pete.

"That's what the scandal was about."

"Griffin was fired for something he never did. and he took the heat in order to —

"To make it all OK for Andi and Mandi and Samantha," said Shirley.

"And I always thought the worst of him," said Pete. Music drifted up from below.

"That's Griffin," said Pete, "and…Denny…and Samantha, and they're playing our song! Let's go."

Down in the main dining room, Andi and Mandi were recovering from the shock of meeting their real father and beginning to understand the good truth about the sacrifices of Donald Griffin. The CAW and the songwriters had joined together in late-night revelry. Pete's old band and the Red Clay Ramblers were belting it out on stage while on the dance floor all the folks freshly saved by Denny Baucom from the evil grip of The Family were joined by writers, poets, musicians, conservatives, reporters and other children of God, singing to the words flashing on the giant screen above the stage.

> Bring your bad side to the bed side
> And your good side, leave behind.
> Our good sides need our bad sides
> To rise above the grind.
> Let's pull the blinds and shake the house
> And let our wild sides shine.
> Bring your bad side to the bed side.
> Darlin', I don't mind.
> And then when comes tomorrow
> A day of sweat and tears
> We'll have our sweet surrender
> To stand against our fears
> The nighthawk watches closely
> As below we start anew.
> Bring your bad side to the bed side.
> Doe-si-doe-op-poo-pe-do.
> Doe-si-doe-op-poo-pe-do.

Late that night, Pete and Shirley cuddled together under the covers.

"I love you, Pete," said Shirley. "If we're together after all this, there is hope."

"And I love you, Shirl."

"Did you love Samantha?"

"Once upon a time. But you know I've learned a lot during these past few crazy days. And one thing I've learned is that you're the only one for me. Samantha and Denny have in some crazy way shown me that the man in me needs the woman in you."

"And the woman in you needs the man in me."

"That sounds like a song. Let's write it together."

"But what do you suppose will happen to Samantha and Denny?" asked Shirley.

"Denny said they're going to Africa with Mandi and Andi and Donald — to meet Tobe — that's Sam's husband, and he —"

"Wait. That's for another book, Pete. Let's just finish this one, first. You haven't had Planting Plot II and I have. And before I forget it, honey, may I ask you one little something."

"Sure, babe."

"Do you think you could stop cleaning your ears with your finger and start using a Q-tip?"

"No problem, babe. Isn't it funny how little things can turn into big things."

"Well, yes. Yes, it is. And that's why I'm going on a diet."

"You know that's not what I meant."

"Pete, I'm glad we can just talk about things. I like it when we talk like this."

"I like it, too, Shirl. It's new for me, but I'm coming to believe that's what it's all about, babe. That's what it's all about."

High above, Hortense folded her wings and headed home — to her nest and warm family.

And in the deep night, after doe-si-doe-op-poo-pe-do, Pete listened through loving, Q-tip clean ears as Shirley, asleep, shouted. "Whap it, boy. Whomp them barbecues. Stomp that snake!"

Afterword
– David Perkins –
The Making of Pete & Shirley

*I*t is risky to do a whodunit without deciding first whodunit, or even whodonewhat. It's even riskier to ask 17 people to write it.

But that's what we did with *Pete & Shirley*, which will go down in history as North Carolina's first and possibly last serial novel, at least until some other editor has the idea of gathering a bunch of writers in his literary pick-up, passing around some moonshine and seeing what happens.

What happened in our case was a lot of laughter and shouting and, when we woke up the next morning — somewhere in Phase II of the Research Triangle Park — a headache or two.

Surely 17 writers and one editor never had more fun — or moaned and groaned more in the process — than the authors of this novel, which ran in daily installments, from Nov. 12 to Dec. 3, 1995, in *The News & Observer*. It might have been easier if we'd asked the United Nations' delegates to write a novel.

Still, no one can blame our writers for an occasional contrariness. The task was really akin to choosing 17 chefs and asking them to prepare the Dream Meal, then telling them that they'd be making up the menu as they went along. And then that they would cook each course without prior consultation.

That wasn't entirely fair, but no one knew that at the start. Least of all the editor.

Pete & Shirley is sheer playfulness. There's sex and politics and religion; clever digs at Cary, Chapel Hill, Durham, Raleigh and the Research Triangle Park; and some memorable characters, including our Tar Heel Everypeople. But *Pete & Shirley* also offers more than one lesson on why novels, generally speaking, should be written by one person.

Every 50 years or so, it seems, an editor forgets this and gets the Great Idea.

The Great Idea for me arrived over dinner with a freind and fellow *N&O* editor, Melanie Sill. "Why don't you all do a novel?" she suggested, referring by "you" to the Features Department. I took her spark: "And maybe we could get all these super-talented writers in our area to do it. And..."I was going a little wild... "they could do it one at a time, you know like that party game, 'Whistle Down the Lane.'"

There is of course a noble history behind novels-in-newspapers, though generally these have been by one author. Dickens' *Pickwick Papers* led the way in 20-install-ments in 1836 and 1837. Thackeray, George Eliot and Hardy all were "periodicized" in newspapers, magazines, or special installments called "part-issues." A recent re-vival of the single-author serial novel was *The Resurrec-tion of Caleb Quine*, which appeared in 1994 in the *Hart-ford Courant*, written by *Courant* staff writer Colin McEnroe.

Serial novels by many hands are nothing new ei-ther. The most famous of recent years was *Naked Came the Stranger,* a soft-core romp written and published as a book in 1969 by a bunch of *Newsday* reporters who set out to spoof the steamy Harold Robbins - style bestseller. They wrote badly — beginning with the first sentence: "Screwed. It was, Gillian realized, an obscene word. But it was the word that came to mind." – on the premise that the public would love it. The public bought 20,000 copies of the book before the hoax was exposed.

Six decades earlier, loftier motives had informed William Dean Howells and *Harper's Bazaar* editor Elizabeth Jordan when they set out on *The Whole Family,* a novel written chapter-by-chapter by 12 authors, including Henry James, Mark Twain, and Howells himself. This high-toned effort ran into trouble with the second chapter when Mary Williams Freeman turned the starchy maiden aunt of Howell's opening into a brazen "modern" woman, raising the gentlemen authors' hackles and forcing them to write around the best character in the book. Her mischief — surely deliberate — was similar to something Jerry Bledsoe did in our novel. (More on that in a minute.) Another story connected with *The Whole Family* is that Henry James refused to follow Mark Twain in the sequence because Twain would be sure to produce a deafening "clareonette solo." *Pete & Shirley* has more than a clarinet; it has a whole jazz band playing as loud as it can.

Unlike Elizabeth Jordan, I had no trouble finding takers for the project. Among the novelists I asked, only Reynolds Price ("No doubt your commitee novel will be interesting"), Doris Betts and Allan Gurganus turned me down. They had too much else to do, they said. I suspect they also knew how similar exercises worked out in their writing classes. Fred Chappell surely knew that too, but he is apparently — and to his credit — game for anything. Of those who agreed, all were enormously enthusiastic.

For his humor and inventiveness, Clyde Edgerton was the obvious choice to open our story. We agreed that the novel would be funny, and that it would be set in the Triangle. But we ran into a minor difficulty right away. The first version of Clyde's chapter was essentially an outline for the entire novel, in fact a plot idea he'd cherished for years. I thought this would reduce the other writers to *sous-chefs* in our crowded kitchen. So I persuaded Edgerton to take Pete and Shirley from the end of his chapter, turn them into primary characters, and to make what happened to Griffin a mystery to be unfolded later.

This move seemed inspired at the time. But, as it

turned out, it created more trouble than a mongoose at a snake-handlers convention. As Clyde observed later, it is impossible to write without knowing where you are going, and our set-up made it impossible for anyone to know where they were going. Perhaps we should have started from the end and written backwards, or perhaps started from both ends at once and met in the middle.

No one wished to take as sacred — or even very seriously — the givens of Clyde's opening chapter. "I'm not going to pull rabbits out of Edgerton's hat!" shouted one writer after I'd pointed out that he hadn't advanced the plot an inch. "Well, somebody's got to pull something from Edgerton's hat!" I countered. He suggested we call a conference. I said I didn't think that would help. Would the writers get together? Could they agree? Wouldn't they just get louder? Finally, Clyde wrote a lovely memo, suggesting directions the novel could take. This was studiously ignored by everybody.

"Look," Lee Smith wrote me consolingly, "if we were anything but individualists, we'd be in offices in Research Triangle Park."

Our writers generally reserved their harshest scorn for their immediate predecessor. "Things were going great until [fill in the name] got to it," was a common phrase. Sometimes this pique was justified. A terrific cliffhanger at the end of one chapter would be a pain in the neck for the next writer, as of course the original writers knew full well, and the next person's instinct was to take revenge by...ignoring it.

Jerry Bledsoe was so impressed with how things were going ("It went all to shit when X got it") that he dumped a handful of wrenches into the works — the biggest wrench being his making Griffin into a secret cross dresser. With a pang, I realized that this was the name of the game, and that the only way to get back at Bledsoe would be to weave it brilliantly into the resolution of the story. This was not easy to do, as the writers had stepped around this supposed cross dresser as gingerly as James and Twain had stepped around Ms. Freeman's bluestocking maiden aunt.

And so our novel zigged and zagged, like the Flying Dutchman's ship, with red herrings flopping in the hold. This was obviously a mystery story, but we were halfway through before anyone added any detail to the underlying story — or what *I* thought was the underlying story. (This was the helpful and obliging Bledsoe). Margaret Maron was so confused when the book arrived on her doorstep, that she had to write a four-page analysis of everything that had occurred, for herself and others. She also added suggestions for directions the novel could take. This too was ignored by everybody, including herself.

For the most part, I played *maitre d'*, trying to keep the paying customers — our prospective readers — happy while the meal was being prepared, and only occasionally going into the kitchen to offer advice: "This character has had a gun in someone's back for three chapters now. Don't you think we should explain WHY?"

Finally, by the end, afraid our wandering ship would never find port, I put on a chef's hat myself and began mixing metaphors. I realized I had to boldly exercise power. The first thing we would do, I said, was stop changing the sex or dress-habits of any character. There would be no new characters, and only one cross dresser. Then I began working on the final scenarios with a playwright and a poet. (Nothing against novelists, actually; I'd simply run out.) For the finale, however, I remembered a generous suggestion of David Guy's — "If Clyde gets to start, he should have to finish!" — and turned again to Clyde, who, as you will have seen, brought us home in his inimitable style. David didn't know that Clyde loves endings.

Once we had a rough idea of the ending, of course, we could go back and make a clearer middle. Margaret Maron said this was how she wrote her mysteries: "I never decide what's going to happen until near the end, and then I always have to go back and rework the middle." We went back to Clyde's and Tim's early chapters and reclaimed Denny, who came to our rescue in more ways than one. Several writers showed noble professionalism and good humor at the end, when several rewrites were required to give the story shape.

Then it was back to the beginning to sprinkle a few foreshadowings: a glimmer of a computer in Chapter One, for example, because the Internet had become important later on. As the deadline bore down, I had what Shirley calls an epiphany. Work like this comes but once in a lifetime.

Of course, we couldn't smooth out every wrinkle, nor did we try. The jumps of logic, the characters' seen from different angles, the "Let's see you get out of this" cliffhangers, the insouciant sidestepping of important details, all reflected the writers' deep reverence for their mission. Perhaps this is something that a serial novel can do well: show us the writing process, the clockwork of storymaking. *Pete & Shirley* is sure to become one of the standard texts of whatever is left of deconstructionism.

It comes down, I suppose, to the essential point that fiction writers create their own universes — and don't much like borrowing someone else's. Still, when it was all over, I felt *Pete & Shirley* had created a world of its own, and I was a little sad to say goodbye to the gang: Pete, Shirley, Monica, Deny and Gloria. I *knew* I would see the evil Braddock again — somewhere.

Under any conditions, it seems, character springs eternal.

Biographies

Clyde Edgerton, who wrote the first and last chapters of *Pete & Shirley*, is the author of six novels: *Raney, Walking Across Egypt, The Floatplane Notebooks, Killer Diller, In Memory of Junior* and *Redeye, A Western.* A Durham-based writer, Edgerton has taught high school and college English and creative writing, most recently at St. Andrews College in Laurinburg, Agnes Scott College in Atlanta and Duke University. He is a member of the Tarwater Band, which specializes in bluegrass, folk and original music.

Lee Smith is the author of 11 books including her most recent novel, *Saving Grace.* She is on leave from North Carolina State University, where she has taught creative writing for more than 20 years. Earlier this year, she received the Lila Wallace-Reader's Digest Fund award, which came with a $105,000 prize. She is married to writer Hal Crowther and they have three children.

Fred Chappell is the winner of numerous prizes for his poetry and fiction, including the Sir Walter Raleigh Prize in 1972 and the Bollingen Prize for Poetry in 1985. He is the author of many volumes of fiction, including *I Am One of You Forever* and *Brighten The Corner Where You Are,* and a new volume of poetry, *Spring Garden.* Chappell is Burlington Industries Professor of English at the University of North Carolina at Greensboro. He also writes about poetry every month as a *News & Observer* book columnist.

111

He lives in Greensboro with his wife, Susan. They have one son.

David Guy is the author of four novels, most recently *The Autobiography of My Body.* He has written articles for various magazines including *Tricycle, New Age Journal* and the *New England Review.* He has also reviewed books for several newspapers including *The New York Times*, *The Washington Post* and *USA Today*. He is also a book columnist for *The News & Observer*. A graduate of Duke University and the father of one son, he lives in Durham with his wife, Alma Blount.

Jill McCorkle is the author of four novels: *The Cheer Leader, July 7th, Tending to Virginia,* and *Ferris Beach,* and one short story collection, *Crash Diet.* Her new novel will be published in the fall of 1996. She received a bachelor's degree in English from the University of North Carolina at Chapel Hill and a master's in creative writing from Hollins College in Virginia. She has taught creative writing at UNC-Chapel Hill, Tufts University, The Bennington Masters of Fine Arts program. Currently she is a Briggs-Copeland Lecturer of Creative Writing at Harvard where she is serving as director of the writing program; she is also serving on the Executive Board of PEN New England. She lives near Boston with her husband and two children.

Tim McLaurin, a Fayetteville native, served in the Marine Corps and toured with a carnival billed as "Wild Bill Mac: The Last Great Snake Show," before putting himself through college at UNC-Chapel Hill, where he earned a journalism degree. He and his wife, Katie, served in the Peace Corps from 1982 to 1984, and McLaurin began writing fiction after their return to the United States. Over the next five years McLaurin's first two novels were published, he and his wife welcomed their second child and McLaurin was offered a teaching position at N.C. State University. In 1989, when he was 35, McLaurin was diagnosed with bone marrow cancer and underwent a bone marrow transplant that cured him of the disease. The author of a memoir and three novels, including *Cured By Fire,* McLaurin lives outside Chapel Hill.

William McCranor Henderson worked as a filmmaker, a rock musician, a radio producer, a freelance journalist, and a screenwriter before he turned to fiction. He was born in Charlotte, raised in Chapel Hill, and is a graduate of Chapel Hill High School and Oberlin College in Ohio. He returned to Chapel Hill in 1989 to teach fiction writing at the University of North Carolina. He now teaches at N.C. State University. He has published two novels, *Stark Raving Elvis* and *I Killed Hemingway,* and is at work on a third, as well as on a memoir of his recent stint as an Elvis impersonator. He is married to writer Carol Henderson and has two daughters, Olivia and Colette.

Kaye Gibbons was born in Nash County in 1960. She graduated from Rocky Mount High School and continued her studies at the University of North Carolina at Chapel Hill. Her first novel, *Ellen Foster,* won the Sue Kaufman Prize for First Fiction from the Academy of Arts and Letters, a Special Citation from the Ernest Hemingway Foundation and the Louis D. Rubin Writing Award from the University of North Carolina. The book has been widely translated and film rights have been sold to New Line Cinema. Her fifth novel, *Sights Unseen,* was published in August. She lives in Raleigh with her husband, Frank Ward, and three daughters and two stepchildren, a son and daughter.

Jerry Bledsoe was a feature columnist for more than 20 years for the Greensboro and Charlotte newspapers. His journalism has won him numerous awards including two National Headliner Awards and two Ernie Pyle Memorial Awards. He's the author of 12 books including *Bitter Blood.* Bledsoe served as contributing editor of *Esquire* magazine from 1972 until 1975. Bledsoe's book *Blood*

Games was made into the CBS movie *Honor Thy Mother* in 1992, and *Bitter Blood* became the CBS mini-series *In the Best of Families* in 1994. His most recent book, *Before He Wakes,* was a finalist for the 1995 Edgar Allan Poe Award. Bledsoe, founder of Down Home Press, publishes non-fiction books about the Carolinas and the South. He and his wife Linda live near Asheboro, N.C. and in Carroll County, Va., where he does most of his writing. They have one son, Erik, who teaches English at the University of Tennessee.

Jaki Shelton Green is a poet and a playwright. Her poems have appeared in women's magazines such as *Essence* and *Ms.* as well as national anthologies such as *Hyperion Poetry Journal, Work Up, Black Poetry of the 80's from the Deep South,* and *The Crucible.* Her books of poetry include *Dead on Arrival,* and *Dead on Arrival and New Poems.* Her play *Blue Opal* premiered in 1994 at the Hayti Heritage Center in Durham. Green was featured last summer in WUNC-TV's "Poetry Live" series. She's currently working on a collection of short stories.

Margaret Maron lives on her family's farm in Johnston County. She's the author of 12 mystery novels and numerous short stories published here and abroad. Her work has been nominated for every major award in the American mystery field. In 1993, her North Carolina-based *Bootlegger's Daughter* won the Edgar Allan Poe Award; the Anthony Award for Best Mystery Novel of the Year; the Agatha Award for Best Traditional Novel; and the Macavity for Best Novel. *Fugitive Colors* was published by Mysterious Press in 1995.

Philip Gerard, a former newspaperman and freelance journalist, has published fiction and nonfiction in numerous magazines including *New England Review/Bread Loaf quarterly* and *The World & I.* He is the author of *Hatteras Light,* a novel, and *Brilliant Passage,* a sailing memoir. His two recent novels are *Cape Fear Rising* and *Desert Kill.* His essays have been broadcast on National Public Radio's "All Things Considered." He has taught at the Bread Loaf Writers' Conference and directs the Professional and Creative Writing Program at the University of North Carolina at Wilmington. He lives in Wilmington with his wife, Kathleen Johnson, and races their sloop "Savior-Faire."

Marianne Gingher is the author of the novel, *Bobby Rex's Greatest Hit* and a collection of stories, *Teen Angel.* A version of *Bobby Rex* entitled *Just My Imagination* was aired in 1992 as an NBC "Movie of the Week," starring Jean Smart and Tom Wopat. In 1987, she was the recipient of North Carolina's Sir Walter Raleigh Award for fiction. She lives mostly on I-40 between Greensboro and Chapel Hill where she teaches creative writing at the university. She is completing two new works of fiction — a book of stories and novellas, and a novel.

Bland Simpson, lecturer in creative writing at the University of North Carolina at Chapel Hill and a member of the Red Clay Ramblers, helped create *Fool Moon,* now playing on Broadway. Simpson's nonfiction novel, *The Mystery of the Beautiful Nell Cropsey* has won a 1995 Historical Fiction Award from the N.C. Society of Historians. With his wife, Ann Cary Simpson, he is at work on a personal portrait of eastern North Carolina.

Laura Argiri is a native of Durham, a novelist, editor and proofreader. Her first novel, *The God in Flight,* was published this year. A graduate of Harvard, she lives in west Durham with three cats.

John Welter was born in Monahans, Texas. He grew up in Oklahoma, Colorado, Kansas and Missouri. He studied English at Longview Community College in Lee's Summit, Mo., and at the University of Missouri-Kansas City, where he earned a bachelor's in English in 1976 and immediately found work in a cafeteria. After working as a copy boy and an obituary writer for *The Kansas City Times*, and as a reporter and columnist for *The Kansas City Star*, he worked for various newspapers in North Carolina and wrote dozens of articles that *The New Yorker* never published. He's the author of two novels, *Begin to Exit Here* and *Night of the Avenging Blowfish.*

Michael Chitwood is the author of two collections of poems, *Whet* and *Salt Works.* His poetry and fiction has appeared in *The Southern Review, Threepenny Review, Poetry, Quarterly West,* and *Virginia Quarterly Review.* He periodically does time in Research Triangle Park, where he writes science articles. He is a regular commentator for WUNC-FM and his book reviews have appeared in Durham's *The Independent, The Charlotte Observer* and *The News & Observer.*

David Perkins has been *The News & Observer*'s book review editor since 1993. He has been a magazine editor in New York City and a reporter for the Anniston (Ala.) *Star.* In the mid-1980s, he covered higher education and state government for *The News & Observer*, winning several prizes from the N.C. Press Association. A classical music critic and a singer, Perkins has also taught journalism and writing at Duke and N.C. State universities. He also edited *The News & Observer's Raleigh: A Living History of North Carolina's Capital,* published in 1995. He lives in Morrisville.